THE SECRET

A Prequel to the Steve Regan Undercover Cop
Thriller Series

Stephen Bentley

Hendry Publishing

BACOLOD CITY, PHILIPPINES

Stephen Bentley/Hendry Publishing
www.hendrypublishing.com
Contact: info@hendrypublishing.com

Publisher's Note: This is a work of fiction. Names, characters, places, and incidents are a product of the author's imagination. Locales and public names are sometimes used for atmospheric purposes. Any resemblance to actual people, living or dead, or to businesses, companies, events, institutions, or locales is completely coincidental.

Cover Art by www.thebookkhaleesi.com
Edited by S. Lee
The Secret/ Stephen Bentley. -- 1st ed.
Print ISBN 978-621-8225-00-8

A huge thank you to all the wonderful team behind my writing. That includes all my beta readers and VIP Readers Group with a special mention for Richard Gonsales-Cavalier who kindly and willingly lent his name to the 'Marmalade' character in this book. I am sure he won't be offended and I believe he may be amused.

Thank you too, Sheryl, for another superb editing job.

Thanks also to Zabrina, my wife, for her continuing unswerving support.

Finally, I thank all you Steve Regan fans for encouraging me to write this prequel. You will be pleased to know a sequel is also planned.

\- Stephen Bentley

"Good things come to those who wait, but only what's left from those who hustle!"

— C.W. Abe Lincoln

CONTENTS

CHAPTER ONE

THE SECRET

There are secrets; there are also big secrets, so massive they cannot be told for many years, if not forever.

My name is Marco. I am the son of Steven Hanrahan. You may know my father better as Steve Regan or even Steve Ryan. He was an undercover cop, one of the best. I had to wrench this story from my father's lips. He told me it was one of the biggest secrets he had ever kept, even from his wife—my mother, who I knew he adored.

Before he told me the full story, which you are about to read, he said, "Son, only tell others this story when the time is right."

That time is now but told by my father, not me. My time will come.

CHAPTER TWO

THEY THINK

It's one of those events that stick in people's minds. Like knowing where you were and who you were with when the whole world thought Britain and America were going to be nuked. JFK had played his cards. Told Khrushchev to get the missiles out of Cuba—*tout suite*. I was fifteen in 1962. I don't think back then I knew the import of "bated breath." Me, and the kids I hung around with on the street corner of a Liverpool housing estate, we expected a nuclear rain to fall. We talked about it—in serious, hushed tones. Most unlike us. We were shitting ourselves. Most of us had seen the government's Civil Defence film about what to expect after the bomb had fallen. Fried where you stood in a fire storm. Burnt toast! Even worse if you weren't close to the firestorm. The radiation cloud would spread for miles contaminating everything – farm animals, crops, the water supply. Eventually humans would die from a slow painful death caused by radiation poisoning. Given a choice, I think I would prefer to be toast. Anyway, the Russians backed down, so we got back to talking about football and the Beatles.

But the event I'm talking about happened four years later. It was the day England won the World Cup. A day that I find impossible to forget and not only because England beat West Germany by four goals to two after extra time. This football match, and one incident in it, played a huge role in my future as an undercover cop.

I am Steven Hanrahan, nineteen, and engaged to be married to Sarah. Her father, Jack, used to be a professional footballer in the lower leagues. Jack and his wife Barbara invited me, my mum and dad over to watch the game at their place. Dad, just for a change, had no shift. He was a traffic cop in Liverpool. The two mums made some sandwiches. Jack got the beers. He worked three nights a week in a local pub so he got a discount. Settling down, we all watched the match, eating the sarnies at half time. Ramsey's 'wingless wonders' were playing well. It was level at half time with England taking the lead after eighty minutes. The nerves jangled. We were all anxious to hear the fulltime whistle, but Germany equalised with one minute to go. Now it was extra time. *More beer, Jack. Thank you.*

Eleven minutes into the first half of extra time, West Ham's Geoff Hurst scored the controversial goal. It was given by the Swiss referee and Russian linesman despite German claims the ball hadn't crossed the line. To me, it seemed like it had. Jack agreed. Dad, being Dad, disagreed. He would often take up the opposite side of an argument whether he believed his point or not. It was his thing. Roger Hunt's immediate reaction convinced me it was a goal. He was a goal scorer, a predator and one of Liverpool Football Club's mainstays. As soon as the ball hit the underside of the crossbar and deflected down into the goal, he simply raised his arm to celebrate and turned away. I knew at that moment he knew it was over the line and therefore a goal. If he was in any doubt, he would have made sure by knocking it over the line as the born goal machine he was.

"Goal!" I shouted, knocking over my beer.

"No goal," Dad said.

I ignored him as did everyone else. We were happy leading in the World Cup Final. The end of extra time came closer. Kenneth Wolstenholme was the BBC commentator. I sat, hardly daring to breathe, willing the Swiss referee to blow for fulltime. Then I heard Wolstenholme: "And here comes Hurst! He's got..." and I wondered, *What's he paused for?* He continued, "Some people are on the pitch! They think it's all over!" Then another short pause until Wolstenholme uttered the immortal words, "*It is now*, it's four!" Geoff Hurst had scored his third and England's fourth goal.

Just like millions of others south of the Border, we danced and cheered. We were deliriously happy. We all went to the pub that night. Jack was working but that didn't stop him quaffing as much beer as me and my dad. Mum, Barbara and Sarah had a good few Babychams too.

I chatted to Brian Barker, Jack's old mate, for a time that evening. He was a bookie with a string of betting shops all over the Liverpool area. He took an interest in my fledgling police career, probably in case he ever needed a future favour. "You fancy being a traffic cop, like your old man? I'd go for the CID if I were you."

"Give me a chance, Brian. I've only just finished my basic training."

My dad didn't like him much because he was often bragging about his money and Jaguar. I think dad had an aversion to Jaguars, not that there were too many of them in our neighbourhood. Tony Kay, an Everton footballer who lived near to us, drove one. He was banned for life from playing football after a match-fixing scandal. Dad sneered every time he saw Kay drive by in the Jag, saying, "There he goes. Picking his nose as always. Ignorant bastard." I used to think, *What's that got to do with Jaguars?*

I made a point of buying one a few years later, mainly to spite my dad. That was my way of getting back at him. It's probably why I married early too. Sarah and I were married in 1969, both of us twenty-two. Too young. But by then I was a detective. Brian was pleased.

CHAPTER THREE

ALONE

After initial training, I walked the beat as all new coppers do. I can't say I enjoyed it. I didn't enjoy wearing a uniform either. It made me feel conspicuous. I prefer blending in rather than standing out. No idea why – I just do. It's me. Perhaps that's what attracted me to the CID, at least subconsciously. Luckily, it didn't take long for me to become a detective. I was twenty-one when I left behind my uniform days – one of the youngest detectives on the force. Within one year, I was a married detective. That, I soon discovered, is not a great combination. Detectives get paid to drink in pubs *sans* wives.

My typical working day as a detective started at 9:00 am at the CID office. Most of the day engaged on case files. Preparing them for both court and for internal records. Fresh or follow-up inquiries could sometimes be conducted over the phone. Sometimes not. On those occasions I would grab a spare CID car, one with no markings, grab a radio and often a colleague and go sleuth. Occasionally even arrest a suspect. Though the start of the day was invariably nine, the usual practice was to go home around one in the afternoon, return to the CID office at three and work for another two hours before returning once more at seven in the evening. We would shuffle paper for a while until 'half brick' time. Someone would call out, "It's that time," then throw an imaginary half brick in the air followed by a cry of, "If it stays up, we carry on with paperwork but if it comes down to earth with a bang, we go to the pub – BANG!"

In my first police station and my first CID attachment, there was a full complement of ten detectives in two teams supervised by two Detective Sergeants each assigned to their team of five. There was a rivalry between the two teams, partly based on religion – or more like bigotry. This was Liverpool and though nowhere near as bad as Northern Ireland, there was a Protestant/Catholic divide. Most of the lads ignored it, but for the sergeants it was serious. It was ironic that I, as a Catholic, was attached to the Protestant sergeant's team. Even more ironic, he later fell in love with and married a Catholic girl – in a Catholic church.

Seven in the evening back in the CID office was time for banter. It was a kind of unspoken jostling for who is going boozing with whom and which pub. The idea in principle was to go drinking to obtain information and meet informants. That did happen, but it was mostly drinking for drinking's sake. I did have an informant to meet by prior arrangement on another day in my life I will never forget. I could have rearranged the meeting, but instead used it as an excuse not to take my wife and daughter to Barbara, my mother-in-law's, home.

By 1969 I was married and had one year under my belt on CID. One year later, Sarah and I were proud parents of Rose, our beautiful daughter. I had also bought a used Jaguar. Things were looking good. But I remember that day in 1970 so clearly. I wish I could turn back time.

"Steve, don't forget we are going to my mum's this evening," Sarah said, smiling.

"Oh, shit. I have an important arrangement for tonight. Can't we put off your mother?"

"Steven Hanrahan…" I always knew she was mad at me if she used my full name, "we made this arrangement over a week ago. Mum has a gift for Rose. I can't put it off."

"Look, Sarah, I have to meet this guy. It could crack a big case I'm working on."

"Tell you what, then. Let me take the Jag, you can get a lift to work."

Before Tony Newland, one of my CID colleagues, picked me up at home that evening I kissed Rose and

Sarah. "See you later tonight, Sarah, and drive safely, eh?"

"I will, and don't wake me up if you have too much to drink."

Twenty minutes later I arrived in the CID office as Sarah drove away from our home on her way to her mother's. Another thirty minutes later, my desk phone rang, "Hello, Detective Constable Hanrahan," I said.

"Hanrahan, come up to see me in my office, please." I knew it was the voice of the uniformed Superintendent, Harry Thomas.

I climbed the one flight of stairs to the top floor of the police station. Before entering the Super's office, I knocked. He called, "Come in."

"Sir, you wanted to see me," I said, walking into his office.

"Sit down, Hanrahan. You want a Scotch or anything?"

Fuck me, this is bad. I know it is.

"Sir, I'd rather you just tell me whatever it is you need to say."

Pouring himself a drink from the Scotch bottle he pulled from a drawer, he said, "Son. This is not easy."

"My wife and daughter…" I think I said but then couldn't speak. My mind became numb. I stared at the pattern on the wallpaper behind the Super trying to figure out the shapes I saw.

I thought I heard him say, *Both killed.*

I woke up the next day in my own bed. I was alone.

CHAPTER FOUR

DREAMS

Sarah had driven the Jaguar into the back of a large truck on the East Lancashire Road. Witnesses told of an explosion followed by a fireball engulfing the Jaguar and the rear of the truck. Fire crews arrived but it was too late. I wasn't interested in seeing any photographs of charred remains. They were no longer human. No flesh and blood left. I no longer felt human in the immediate aftermath. At first, I refused to accept it had happened at all. Then, I blamed myself for working when I should have been driving my wife and daughter. The third phase was anger. I was angry with the world. There was no god in my heart anymore. How could there be a god when he allowed such innocents to be killed? My mother and grandmother remonstrated with me over my abandonment of my faith. I didn't care. They were the only two living women in the world who I loved. Sarah, the third, was now dead. Rose, dead. I would never see her grow into a woman. There were no angels. No heaven, no god, nothing. Unless you call a void and a pain in my heart something and not nothing.

The two dads were there and Barbara. Barbara soon cottoned on I needed to be left alone. My dad and Sarah's dad, Jack, didn't know what to say or do. That was fine by me. They also knew I wanted to be alone in the house. My private moments were when I got drunk at home, shouted, screamed, invoked God's name to strike me down dead if he wanted to prove he existed. I railed at religion. I railed at the world. It was a trick – a huge hoax. Happiness was a mirage. I drank myself to sleep most nights, smelling Sarah's scent on the bed sheets. I also hugged Rose's blanket to me. I could smell my precious baby. I cried, unashamedly sobbed, until sleep arrived and dreams. Dreams that would never come true, but they kept Sarah and Rose alive in my heart and mind.

CHAPTER FIVE

THE RUMOUR

I didn't work for six months. The family doctor kept renewing the sicknotes. I didn't even have to go to see him. I called the surgery and the receptionist would tell me to come pick it up the next day. Tony Newland used to collect it from my home after I called the office. There was no conversation when I called on the phone. I would hear, "Steve, how are you?"

I'd say, "You know …" followed by silence. It was code for tell Tony to get my sicknote. Tony never stayed long. The silence was awkward for both of us.

The two mums would visit but only after they first called me to ask if it was convenient. They came separately as if they had worked out a roster. They cooked, cleaned, washed my clothes and the bedding, but not once did they interfere with the clothing or any belongings of Sarah or Rose. That was important to me. I still used Sarah's clothing to remind me of her smell. My daughter's blanket was tucked away under my pillow. They both knew. Not once did they move it or suggest washing it. Mum held me close a few times. I sobbed. She cried too as she wiped my eyes and cheeks with a handkerchief. None of my visitors spoke much. They knew I had nothing to say. Those who loved and knew me recognised I needed time to heal.

I'd been off work for around three months when I heard the doorbell ring. I was surprised to see Brian Barker at the front door but asked him in. I guess I shouldn't have been too surprised. He treated Sarah like his own daughter and by extension, me as a son. He'd never had any kids so I think we were his surrogates.

His smiling face was what I needed. Enough sorrow. "Brian, come in. Good to see you," I said and meant it.

"Detective Steve Hanrahan, I presume," he said and laughed. "Too early?" He flourished a bottle of Scotch.

"Nope. I'll get two glasses. Sit down." He knew where to find the living room from the last time he'd visited. We settled into our respective armchairs after he'd poured two stiff drinks from the bottle of single malt. I took a big slug, sighed then said, "Tastes good."

I have no idea why my old man never liked Brian. He was smart in a street kind of way. I suppose he had to be given he was a bookmaker. I sensed he'd heard the sigh and was going to tread lightly. I was right.

"Steve, you will find answers in your own time. I'm not here to give you any bullshit about getting back to work to take your mind off everything. I hope you do go back because you are a fucking good detective. You'll know when it's time."

This was another reason I liked him. He told it as it was. He was a straight talker. No riddles and no hidden agenda.

"Brian, I appreciate that, I really do. I know I will go back. As you say, it's just a matter of when, not if."

"Good. Now, have you heard the rumour?"

"What rumour?"

"The ref and the linesmen in the World Cup final were bribed."

"You're kidding me."

"I'm not. When you are back at work we'll talk again, okay?"

"Sure thing."

We had another couple of drinks before he left. Hugging me on his way out, he said, "Take care, son." I swear there was a tear in his eye.

I slept well. The first time in months. There was no anger. I was intrigued by the rumour but I also needed more time-out. Time to rest, heal and get ready for the future. So I called my brother in Canada and he simply said, "Get on that plane, right now."

It wasn't quite 'right now' as I had to get the okay from my boss for a year-long sabbatical on top of my six month's sick leave.

CHAPTER SIX

LONDON CALLING

Now, I was ready for the fray having returned from Canada feeling a year older but also brand new. I soon started to pick up from where I had left off, at least from a work perspective.

Brian Barker had connections in high places. He was a Freemason and used his network within that secretive organisation whenever it suited him. It was no secret that many police officers of all ranks were Freemasons. I had no interest in becoming a mason for one simple reason. This was a network where favours were asked and given. To me, that compromised integrity, or could do. I wasn't prepared to find out. My job as a detective was simple: I gather evidence, arrest the suspect, interrogate and charge him, put together an evidence file, then leave the rest to the lawyers and courts. It was uncomplicated. It also helped in that I was never a cynic. I do think if a detective is cynical, they are more likely to bend the law to ensure a conviction. I was never comfortable with that as it sometimes led to wrongful convictions and miscarriages of justice. It was a perversion of the system and of the human condition.

Brian heard I was back and knew it was time for me to return to work. I had been absent for over one year. Before my trip to Canada, he had been checking in on me at home every week since the first visit. Not once had he mentioned the rumour again until now.

"You're looking and sounding much better, Steve," Brian said as he fell into the armchair in my living room.

"I feel better. Much better. In fact. I know I'm ready to return to work."

"Can I talk to you about that?"

"Brian, you can talk to me about anything."

"How do you fancy working undercover?"

"What, as a spy kind of thing?"

"Precisely."

"So, who are you really? 'M' from one of the Bond movies? You are certainly not Miss Moneypenny."

We both laughed. "Nothing like that. But you know I'm in the funny handshake mob?"

"A mason, yes. I know."

"Well, I happen to know you can get a transfer to London working on a really hush-hush project. But only if you want it."

"What project?"

"You know – the rumour."

"The World Cup?" I said after recalling his earlier conversation.

"Yes. It's all very sensitive but the Home Secretary has instructed the Metropolitan Police Commissioner to investigate."

"How do you know all this if it's so secret?"

"Freemasons, son. The Home Secretary's a top mason as is the Met Commissioner."

"But how do you have your ear so close to the ground on what's going on in London?"

"I don't, but a bookie friend of mine does, Terry Culver. He told me. That's where I first heard this rumour. He's crapping himself."

"Why, exactly?"

"He was part of the plan, the bribe."

"Hmm, sounds interesting, but how come you are certain I'd become involved? They must have under-cover guys in London."

"They need someone from outside. The Met Commissioner is a good friend of the Liverpool Chief Constable, your boss. I'm a good friend of his."

"This has been discussed already?"

"Yes, and it's yours if you want it, Steve. It's up to you, son."

One week later I was seated in the CID HQ office, a part of the Liverpool City Police HQ building, talking to the Assistant Chief Constable (Crime), Mister Topping.

"How's your dad, Hanrahan?"

"Fine thanks, sir."

"Best copper we got on the Traffic Division. More crime arrests than some detectives. I'm glad you chose the CID."

I didn't answer. I was pondering, *Is this about my father or me?*

Hearing no response, Topping asked in his deep gruff voice, "Right lad, the quacks say you're fit to return to work but how do you feel about that?"

"I'm fine, sir. It's time for me to get back in the saddle, so to speak."

"You want me to arrange a transfer to the mounted section? Only kidding… look, Hanrahan, the Chief has asked me to sound you out on something."

"Sir?"

"How do you fancy working down in the smoke for a while?"

"The smoke… London?"

"Yes."

"Depends."

"Well… that's the problem. It's all very secret squirrel – hush hush, you know. Even the Chief doesn't know the details and I'm buggered if I do if the Chief doesn't.

"Hmm… intriguing."

"You could say that. Here's a suggestion – why don't you go meet with the Metropolitan Police Commissioner at Scotland Yard? After he's clued you in, then you can decide, eh?"

"That sounds sensible to me. What happens to my old CID job here if I decide not to go to London on this secret mission?"

"Son, now you're sounding like 007. Your job is always here for you. You are one of the brightest young detectives we have."

"That's that, then. Thanks. I'll go and find out what they want me to do. Is that all, sir?"

"Yes, son, and… be careful.

CHAPTER SEVEN

THE COMMISSIONER

Brian was right. The meeting with Sir Edward Reid, the Met Commissioner, went well. We met in his office in Scotland Yard. Only the two of us. He told me about the bribe involving bookmakers and the World Cup officials. He asked me if I was willing to go undercover to gather information and, hopefully, some evidence. All the time he stressed how sensitive and confidential this task was. I was to report directly to him and only at his home, never in Scotland Yard. He gave me his private direct numbers both in Scotland Yard and his home. I was to remain a serving police officer but with my own force, not the Met. He did say I would be paid extra allowances: one was a London living allowance and the other was an enhanced rent allowance. Both designed to help me cope financially with the higher costs of living in the capital.

Following his briefing, Sir Edward said, "Any questions?"

"Only two. First, why me?"

"You're honest, from outside, and I'm told you are a damn fine young detective. Also, you are not a Freemason. Second question?"

"When do I start?"

"As soon as possible, Steve. By the way and I should have said it earlier, I'm sorry about your wife and daughter. Terrible thing."

"Thank you, sir. I appreciate it. I think this assignment is just what I need. It will help," I said.

"Before you leave, one more thing."

"Sir?"

"When this is finished, think about joining the Freemasons. It helps on the promotion ladder."

"Thanks for the advice, sir, and no offence but I don't think it's right promotions should be influenced by secret societies."

Sir Edward smiled, walked over to my side of his large desk and shook my hand. I could feel the extra pressure he applied to two of my knuckles – *funny handshake*, I thought.

I started to leave his office when I heard him speak again. "Steve, sorry, I nearly forgot and it's important. You'll need a false name for your undercover role. I suggest you keep your first name, just change your family name. Any thoughts?"

I was deep in thought, gazing at the rows of old framed photographs on the wall. That's when it came to me. "Regan, R-E-G-A-N, sir. Regan sounds good."

"Yes, but I think it's pronounced *Raygun* not *Reegan*. Regan with only one 'a' - it's the Irish way."

"*Raygun*. I like it."

"I'm curious. Why Regan?"

I nodded to an old photo on the wall. A certain Herbert Regan was Commissioner of the Metropolitan Police in 1873.

Gazing out of the taxi window, making my way back to Euston station for my Liverpool train, I spoke to the cab driver. "Is it always this busy?"

"Scouse, this is the smoke. I take it you're from Liverpool?"

"Yeah."

"Let me put it his way. I reckon you can fit five cities the size of Liverpool into London. Good team, though."

"Everton or Liverpool?"

"Both… but not as good as the Hammers. We won the World Cup, you know?"

"With a bit of help from Roger Hunt."

"Suppose… but Bobby Moore, Martin Peters and of course Geoff Hurst – the backbone of West Ham and England."

I smiled. Little did he know.

CHAPTER EIGHT

IN FOR A PENNY

My home in the Liverpool suburbs was rented out. With the help of the two mums and dads, the rooms were emptied. Aside from clothing, I had decided to take nothing with me – a clean break – except for some framed photos and Rose's bed blanket. I told the family to keep what they wanted and to make sure the remainder found a good home.

It was also a clean break from the CID office. There was no traditional farewell piss-up when a detective was transferred, seconded, or left the job to take a pension. That suited me. No need to talk about anything - me, Sarah, Rose or where I was going. I did see Mister Topping at CID HQ again. He handed me a large padded and sealed envelope addressed to me. I handed him an envelope containing my warrant card identifying me as Detective Constable Steve Hanrahan. On completion of the exchange, he said, "Good luck, Steve."

I stayed in a hotel in Liverpool City Centre that night. It was convenient for Lime Street Station for my train to London the following day. Opening my package in the hotel room, I went through the contents. It contained the new me. I had a new driving licence, National Insurance ID card, school certificates, and job references, all in the name of Steve Regan. More important was a copy of an introduction letter addressed to Terry Culver asking Culver to find work for Regan. It was signed: *'Your Dear Friend, Brian Barker.*

So, Brian's in on this too, thought the new Regan.

I had checked in as Steve Regan owing to Topping having arranged and paid for the one-night stay. All cash. There was no way to trace it all back to the HQ CID. I was reborn, or that's what it felt like. I was excited too at the prospect of this mission, as my mind insisted on calling it.

The excitement grew on the train journey to London. A degree of apprehension accompanied the excitement. I kept drumming the new name into my head, as well as the names of the schools and jobs detailed in the papers I carried in my hold all. I could see my new suitcase in the rack. It bore a stencil of 'S Regan.' *In for a penny, in for a pound*, I kept believing. I was also thinking, *I bet I'm one of the first undercover cops in this country.* I certainly wasn't aware of any others.

I read the newspaper to kill some time then started on an Ed McBain 87th Precinct paperback. The last stop before London Euston was Milton Keynes. I closed my eyes when the train pulled away, soon mesmerised by the sound of iron wheels hurtling along iron tracks. I had no idea how long I'd been napping, but on looking out of the train window to my left, I could see Wembley's twin towers. The sight snapped me into focus. Wembley, 1966, the World Cup. *That's why I'm here*, I thought. I started to get nervous.

It took the train another fifteen minutes or so to come to a halt at Platform Seven at London's Euston Station. I spent that time opening and reopening my wallet. I kept checking the new Steve Regan driving licence, looking for flaws. There weren't any. I then unfolded a piece of paper. It was torn out of a small notebook. The paper was lined and folded in half. I kept reading, trying to commit Brian Barker's handwriting to memory. Stupid, really, as I had no need. It's what nerves do to a person. The note from Brian contained Terry Culver's address.

CHAPTER NINE

TERRY CULVER

Terry, baptised Terence Patrick Aloysius Culver, the eighth child of Patrick and Marie Culver, was a sick child. It was not until his fourteenth birthday he started to gain weight and develop muscles. His father claimed the credit, telling all who cared to listen it was his insistence that young Terry started boxing. Terry was born and raised in Whitechapel, so it was natural he enrolled at the famous Repton Boxing Club in nearby Bethnal Green. He soon made a name for himself in the flyweight division, securing an Amateur Boxing Association winner's medal at under-17 level. He also befriended gangsters there.

He was no stranger to illegal activities as a teenager. Before the overhaul of England's betting laws, he was a bookie's runner for his father, collecting betting slips and the wagers mainly from Irish labourers employed at London building sites. His quickness of foot saw him escape from the police on several occasions, still clutching the slips and wads of cash.

On completion of his National Service in the Army, he knew what he had to do. The government had legalised betting shops in 1961. Together with his father, he opened one of the new betting shops in Walthamstow, East London. It was estimated ten thousand new betting shops opened throughout the country within the first six months of them becoming legal. Within six years of the first Terry Culver Turf Accountant shop opening, Terry had opened another twenty all over east and south London. His father insisted the shops carry his son's name as he wished to take a back seat in the business. Terry was devastated when his father suddenly died the week before the twenty-first shop was opened. Its location was in the same street Terry was born in Whitechapel.

Terry and Brian Barker first met in the Army while both were doing their National Service. They got on well. Both had a shared passion for horse racing and betting. Together, they ran an illegal betting operation within their unit. The officers turned a blind eye. They had stayed in touch ever since those days, often using each other as sounding boards. Brian had also successfully opened a string of betting shops in and around Liverpool. As well, they were both Freemasons. Brian and Terry ran with the hares and the hounds. They knew as many gangsters as they knew police officers. Both criminals and coppers were part of the secretive

Freemason society. Terry was well known in his London Lodge, as was Brian in his Liverpool Lodge. Freemasonry served a purpose for both bookmakers. It was also an opportunity for both men to meet on an annual basis at the Grand Master's Banquet in London's Great Queen Street.

Steve Hanrahan, now Regan, was still a wet-behind-the ears twenty-four-year old detective. He knew nothing of Brian's and Terry's connections other than Terry was somehow involved in the rumour about the World Cup bribe.

Terry Culver's home was a five-bedroom detached house in Wanstead. Three weeks before Steve Hanrahan set off in the train to London as Steve Regan, Culver was at home. He picked up the phone, shooing his wife away. "Brian, me old mate, how the fuck are yer?"

"Good, Terry, I'm good. Business is great. Life is good. What more can a man ask for?"

"What can I do you for? It's not Grand Master's Banquet time so I guess you need something."

"Bloody hell, Terry, you can read me like a book. Yeah, I'm after a favour but not really for me… for an old family friend."

"Is it about the letter you sent me?"

"Yes."

"Okay, my man. Tell me more and I'll see what I can do."

Three weeks to the day after that phone call, a black London cab dropped me off at Culver's home in Wanstead. I knew about the letter, Brian's phone call and that Culver was expecting me. Apart from that, and they were close friends, I knew little else.

I was in awe on first seeing Culver's home. It was more like a mansion. I was kind of expecting a Batman-style butler to appear at the front door and was a bit surprised to see a middle-aged guy with greying hair, wearing a dark blue suit, open the front door. I felt he looked a bit like Terry Thomas in those films where Thomas played the upper-class bounder, except there was no gap in this man's teeth and no posh accent. I knew that as soon as he opened his mouth to speak.

"You must be Steve. Come in, boy." He had a distinct Cockney accent and added, "Brian's told me all about you."

"I am," was all I could say before he showed me through into a large living room off to the left of the hall. The room was well-furnished with paintings of racehorses decorating the walls. Culver invited me to sit in a huge leather armchair. I accepted as I admired the racehorses.

"You like them?" Culver asked.

"Yeah. Beautiful," I said. "Your horses?"

"Nah! Those nags made me a fortune. They were all heavily backed and lost. But I won… big time." Culver chuckled. "Fancy a gold watch?"

I glanced at my stainless-steel watch and saw it was six in the evening. I must have looked puzzled as Culver realised I wasn't familiar with Cockney rhyming slang.

"Scotch. Gold watch, get it?" He was still laughing as he reached a large drinks cabinet a few yards away. He poured two generous helpings of Scotch into ornate cut-glass tumblers before offering me one.

"Thanks," I said.

"Single malt. The finest."

I took a sip and it tasted smooth. I nodded in approval.

"Glad you like it. Marmalade brought it back on his last trip home to Dundee."

"Marmalade?"

"Yeah, everyone calls him that on account of his red hair and he's from Dundee."

"Jam, jute and journalism. The three J's. That's what Dundee is famous for. See, I did learn something at school," I said.

"Marmalade ain't jam though," Culver said.

"Maybe, maybe not? It's made from fruit though."

"Yeah, you got me there."

"So, what's Marmalade's real name?"

"Dick. Dick Cavalier. He chauffeurs me around sometimes. You'll probably meet him tomorrow at the office. Talking about tomorrow, you've had a long trip. Finish off that Scotch and we start in the morning."

"Fine by me, thanks."

"Don't call him Marmalade to his face, though. He's got a temper to match the colour of his hair."

"Got it, Mister Culver."

"Terry, son, call me Terry."

We chatted for another hour or so before Mrs Culver came in the room. It was mostly about betting, but nothing was said about football betting or the World Cup. I also rehearsed my back story about how I knew Brian Barker. Culver seemed happy about that, especially the part about Brian and my dad being good mates. That wasn't true, as you know. Nothing about Steve Regan or my back story was true apart from my first name, and I was from Liverpool.

"Steve, so good to meet you," Mrs Culver said offering her hand.

I shook it, saying, "Likewise, Mrs Culver."

"Rene, it's Rene." She smiled. "Let me show you where your bedroom is before we eat dinner."

"Forgot to mention that, Steve," Terry Culver said. "We'll find you some digs once you find your way around. You'll want some privacy, no doubt. Your own space."

I nodded without speaking. I was envisioning 'dinner.' Dinner in Liverpool is what you eat at midday'ish. Tea, maybe supper, is what you eat at this time of day. Terry must have considered me rude when I didn't respond. I followed Mrs Culver up the stairs, still deep in thought. *Dinner? Tea? Supper? Gold watch? This is all going to take some getting used to.*

"Here we are, the guest room." Mrs Culver's voice snapped me out of my thoughts. I looked to my right down the landing. It seemed like there were three bed-rooms on that side of the house. The guest room was built on top of the garage below. She showed me in to what was going to be my temporary home. It was clean, comfortable, and had a single bed, chest of drawers, and an armchair. Between them, they almost filled the room. She walked across to another door on the far side of the bedroom. It opened up into a space to hang clothes and off to the right was a shower enclosure and a huge bathtub – one of those with the ornate legs. "Clean towels there," Mrs Culver pointed to a shelf, "and your dirty laundry basket is there," she indicated to me. "Pauline, my house helper, will check it and do your laundry."

Perhaps it is a mansion? I thought. *House helper and chauffeur. Welcome to another world, Steve.*

After thanking Mrs Culver, she and I returned downstairs to join Terry in the dining room. He was sitting at the dining table. A plump fifty-something lady dressed in a black uniform with a white apron at the front was busying herself with bringing in serving plates stuffed with meat and vegetables. *Pauline,* I thought, and smiled inwardly as Mrs Culver said, "This is Pauline. This is our guest, Pauline, Mister Steve Regan."

"Hello," I said and smiled.

Pauline returned a two-syllable hello in curt fashion without any sign of emotion. *Please yourself*, I felt.

There was more small talk around the table as I devoured the roast beef and vegetables. I learnt Pauline cooked it all. She had a cooking apron and the pristine starched white serving apron I saw when she served. She did the lot, cooking, much of the cleaning, and the laundry. Another lady came in twice a week to help with the cleaning duties.

We also drank some fine red wine. It made me feel tired so I excused myself after dinner to grab some sleep in my room.

I liked Mr and Mrs Culver. That feeling was reinforced the following morning. I wondered if my real purpose in being here – if successful – was going to haunt me in years to come. I hoped not.

CHAPTER TEN

NEW BOY

Mrs Culver took me to my first day's work at the head office of Terry Culver Turf Accountants in Barking. First, she cooked me a breakfast of bacon and eggs which I wolfed down.

"Terry said to let you have a lay-in," she explained. "I usually start at ten so it's no big deal. Marmalade drove him in, as usual."

"What do you do there, Mrs Culver?"

"Rene, please. I cook the books," she said with a grin.

"Well, if you cook them like you cook brekkie, then all's good." We both laughed.

"I'm only joking. I'm the bookkeeper. I get all the stuff ready for the accountant. He's the one who cooks the books... no... I'm joking."

I made my mind up early about Mrs Rene Culver. She was too nice to be involved with bribes or anything to do with rigging football matches. *Mind you, so is Terry*, I thought – almost chastising myself for not staying open-minded to all possibilities. *Greed isn't the sole preserve of unlikeable people,* I reminded myself.

"You want me to wash the dishes, Mrs... I mean, Rene?"

"Goodness, no. Pauline will clear up after we leave for work. Are you ready?"

"Ready and willing but a little nervous," I said with a smile.

I followed her out through the front door as far as the souped-up Vauxhall Viva parked in the drive. It was British Racing Green and sported the Jack Brabham insignia that differentiated it from the common-or-garden models. No sooner had I got comfortable in the front passenger seat than Rene beamed with pride and introduced me to her "trusty steed." Her choice of car seemed incongruous on first impression, but I soon learned it's fatal to judge a book by its cover. She gunned it through Wanstead, then along the North Circular Road as if determined to win the British Grand Prix. I had to admire not only her driving skills but also the throaty roar of the race-inspired Brabham Viva. My chariot driver smiled from ear to ear each time she overtook any car in front of her. It was as if it was a gross affront to her pride to be second, never mind third in this game of imaginary championship racing. *She's a winner*, I thought.

The race, I mean journey, took no time at all. I noticed the Barking exit sign and as she turned off the busy North Circular, I confess I heaved a small sigh of relief on her slowing down somewhat. The scenery had not been much more than a blur, but sufficient for me to start to comprehend the vastness of the capital city. I noted the contrasts between the sedate leafy suburbs like Wanstead and the more cheek to jowl housing of areas such as Walthamstow and Ilford. The haves, have-nots, want-some-of-it by fair means or foul, and the couldn't-give-a-shit types were all habitués of this sprawling landscape. It was just that at that moment, I didn't know it. I was at the start of a lifelong learning curve about people.

My immediate task was to learn more about Terry, his business, and staff including Marmalade – *note to self: must not say that to his face*. Rene first introduced me to the staff on the ground floor, those taking bets enclosed behind a huge plain glass screen. An old guy who looked a bit like a tramp dressed in dirty old clothes including stained raincoat and soiled trousers called out in a gruff Irish accent, "Pleased to meet yer sonny, are you new?"

Rene intervened before I could speak. "Miles, give him a chance to settle in, won't you?"

I took my cue from her. "Yes, Miles, I'm new. My name's Steve. Good to meet you." He smiled as if he wasn't used to people noticing him. It was then I saw his dog by his side. It was a small terrier that looked far cleaner than his owner. "Yours?"

"It is. Terry lets me bring it in the betting shop. He's no trouble, is he, Mrs C?"

"That's true, Miles, except when he sees Marmalade."

"Haha! That is so. I dunno what it is about that fella, but Samson here does not like him one bit."

I gathered two things: Marmalade must be elsewhere with Terry for him to be referred to by his nickname, and Miles had a sense of humour calling a tiny mutt Samson.

"I'll be seeing you, then," I said as I followed Rene through the now unlocked door which led to the office upstairs by way of the private area behind the screen. A young woman had let us through the door so we could access the screened off area out of bounds to the public. She was pretty with a nice smile. I smiled back and softly said, "Hi." She blushed.

Rene noticed all this. "Margaret, this is Steve. Steve, Margaret."

I said, "Hi," again and she blushed even more this time.

Terry was sitting in a large swivel chair, I guess it was termed an 'executive chair,' inside his office on the first floor of the building. It was a dark room, sombre really, with fake pine cladding on every wall. The walls were decorated with framed family photos as well as Chamber of Commerce accolades praising

Terry Culver for his undoubted business acumen. The sunlight was excluded by way of a closed Venetian blind at the window overlooking the busy high street. There was an overhead light slung from the ceiling, encased in a cheap glass chandelier fitting, and a desk light too, but they did little to alleviate the sobriety of the office.

Rene showed me in then left us alone. The 'us' was me, Terry, and a man who was obviously Marmalade judging by his shock of red hair. I glanced at him. He glared at me. It was a classic case of mutual instant dislike. I could almost touch the feeling. Terry knew, too. I heard his nervous cough before he spoke.

"Steve, welcome. Take a seat. By the way, this is Dick. Dick Cavalier, my chauffeur and helper."

I graciously but reluctantly nodded in Marmalade's direction to acknowledge his presence but refused to speak his name. Marmalade on his part simply ignored me.

"Thanks, Terry, I will," I said, reminding myself not to call the red-haired Scot by his nickname though I was sorely tempted.

"How was the drive here?" Terry Culver laughed. I knew what he was referring to.

"Quick," I said, echoing his laughter. I again glanced at the Scot. There was no expression on his face at all. I resisted the temptation to ask him if he hailed from the City of Granite rather than Dundee considering his stony visage.

"Fancy a drink?" Terry said holding up a bottle of malt whisky.

With a quick but needless glance at the wall clock that seemed to loom just above Terry's head, I said, "Too early for me."

Terry poured himself a wee dram but as "wee" as it was, I began to suspect he had an alcohol problem. It was only ten-thirty in the morning.

The Scot said, "May I?"

"Help yourself wee man," Terry said.

There was nothing wee about Dick Cavalier. He was a hulking giant of a man, easily six-feet-four inches tall with shoulders as wide as the River Clyde. *Cavalier by name and cavalier by nature*, I thought. *A chauffeur hitting the bottle at this time of day.*

As he savoured the whisky, Terry gave me a quick verbal tour of the business, in between sipping the golden liquid. I noticed Marmalade had slung his down his throat in one gulp. "Right, Steve. Downstairs is where the action takes place. You may have met some of the staff already and possibly one of our best punters, Miles. He looks like a tramp and has a little dog but don't let his looks fool you. He's one of the wealthiest people in Barking. He's just canny, as Dick here would say, with his money. He's a feisty old fucker too, used to be in the Marines… commando, some say. Let's put it this way. He's the only punter I would allow to bring a pet onto the premises."

"More's the pity," Marmalade muttered loud enough to hear.

"It's not the mutt's fault he doesn't like you. It must be that Scottish blood."

"Aye, Sassenach mutt!"

Terry and I laughed. Even Marmalade saw the funny side and joined in.

Terry continued, "Right, where was I? Yes, we take the bets and pay out downstairs. The day's takings are reconciled then placed in the safe in that same screened off staff area. That is holy ground. No one except me, Rene, and staff are allowed in there. You are too, seeing you are staff now."

"What have you got in mind for me? Work, I mean."

"Dunno yet. Something will come to mind. Let's get you settled in first, eh?"

"Suppose, at least until I start to get the hang of the business."

"How does fifteen quid a week sound?"

I heard Marmalade cough, more of a slight choking noise, but ignored him. "Sounds fine to me, Terry."

"Good. Cash in hand, every Friday. I'll make sure Rene knows and keep you off the books. The less the taxman knows, the better."

I nodded in agreement, thinking, *The less people know about me, the better all round.*

Terry noticed me looking at the map on the wall. It had red marker pins stuck in it. "In case you are wondering, that's the Terry Culver Turf Accountants empire. Each pin is one of my betting shops."

"Wow!" I remarked. "So, how many people work for you in all?"

"About sixty. The accountant will know exactly because they are all on the payroll except you and Dick here."

"That's some achievement," I said and meant it. I saw Terry's chest fill with pride.

"Thanks," Terry said. "Why don't you go have a wander around downstairs? Watch and learn kind of thing. Later today you can come with me and Dick to a piss up in a pub. A bit of business I need to see to."

"Good idea," I said.

I stood and left the office, ignoring Marmalade, and he reciprocated. *I need to be careful with him*, I imagined.

CHAPTER ELEVEN

RUNNERS AND RIDERS

The rest of the day at the Barking betting shop and headquarters of the Terry Culver Turf Accountants empire went without incident. I was introduced to Shirley – she paid out on winning bets, and Moira who looked after the "blower" – the transmission system that fed live from the racecourses so the punters could hear live progress on their chosen nags. She was also responsible for making sure the *Racing Post* pages for the day were fixed to the walls in the shop. That was for the punters who wanted to check the runners and riders, weights, and all the other bits of info to do with form and help them choose a winner. Me? A pin was what I would use. She had the added task of making sure there were plenty of blank pads of betting slips stashed in the little wooden boxes nailed to each wall above the wooden ledge where most punters scribble out their selected bets.

I also met Derek. He oversaw the whiteboard on which he scrawled the name of the racecourse, the time of the next race and the odds for each runner. He was a serious chap in his mid-thirties with black hair forming a widow's peak. I suspected he dyed his hair to hide any premature greying. I don't know why I believed that. It just seemed so.

Margaret remained just as shy but smiled at me a lot. I started to feel like a village idiot because as much as I returned her smiles, she failed to talk to me. It was a little unnerving. I had no idea what her function was. Perhaps she was backup to the others? If one went missing in the line of duty, Margaret would step in guns blazing, shedding her demure appearance like some mythical Amazonian super heroine. The notion turned me on. She was attractive with long blonde hair, sparkling blue eyes, and bumps and curves in all the right places. *I think I'll ask her out on a date when I get my own pad*, I thought.

At break times, I was soon introduced to the culinary differences between the capital, or 'Smoke' as we Scousers call it, through my desire to taste a saveloy - a type of sausage made from pork brains, usually bright red, and normally boiled. I wish I hadn't bothered. I found them tasteless. I stuck to my fish n' chips mainly but did enjoy pie and mash with the green liquor. That was worth discovering.

The time passed quickly. I was just starting to feel comfortable when Terry and Marmalade entered the back office. I had heard them coming down the creaking stairs that connected the ground to the first floor.

"C'mon, Steve. We're off to the boozer." That was all he said, and I didn't need a second invitation. You know what they say about a change of scenery. As I followed the two men to the Jaguar I saw Marmalade's feet, or to be exact, the way he walked. His feet were splayed out, pointing to different parts of the compass. His right foot pointed North East. The left to North West. I had this peculiar image in my mind of him standing in the middle of Liverpool Pier Head, back to the river, watching the sun rise with his right foot pointing to Halewood and the left to Kirkby. *Perhaps those saveloys were psychedelic?*

Shrugging off this image, I jumped into the backseat of the Jaguar with Marmalade behind the steering wheel and Terry in the front passenger seat. The car was soon on the North Circular heading south. That was when Terry spoke again. "Got your passport, I hope."

He swivelled in his seat and must have seen the expression on my face. It was one of puzzlement, but it concealed an inner panic. Panic because I thought, *I have false documents for most things but not a passport*. My panic disappeared when he burst into laughter. "Blimey! You should have seen your face.

We're off to south London, across the river. It's a joke, Steve."

All I could muster was, "Oh, okay." I felt a bit foolish. Thank goodness Marmalade kept his cakehole shut as he drove the Jag on through Poplar then through the Blackwall Tunnel. I didn't know it then, but we were on the way to a pub in Bermondsey.

About thirty minutes out of the south side of the tunnel, we arrived at the Bricklayers Arms in Bermondsey. It was immediately apparent both Terry and Marmalade were familiar with the place. As we walked through the large lounge bar at the front, Marmalade stopped to talk to five men seated around a table drinking beers and whiskey chasers. "One minute, Terry. I'll just catch up with me old mates for a mo," Marmalade said in his thick Scottish accent. Terry, for his part, threw up a hand in a gesture of understanding as well as agreement.

As Terry and I walked towards a bar at the back of the pub, he whispered to me, "Mark my words, young Steve. That team of blaggers will have Marmalade back in the nick as sure as eggs is eggs. Bloody fool."

I knew blaggers was London criminal slang for armed robbers. The most active of them were based in south London, specialising in robbing security vans, wearing black nylon stockings over their heads and using sawn off shotguns to intimidate the guards.

I was curious about one thing. "What do you mean 'back in the nick'?"

"He's on parole, having served six years out of a nine stretch. I was the only one who would employ him."

"I see." I was starting to see Terry as a kind man who would lend a helping hand to those in need like Marmalade. Indeed, like me, but only because of Brian's lies cementing my back story.

I believe this was the first time I knew that just because a person breaks the law, it doesn't necessarily follow that makes them a bad person. It was also the first time I had some reservations about deceiving people with my duplicity.

My reflections were interrupted as soon as Terry and I entered the back bar. There was a loud shout of, "Well, fuck me, if it ain't Batman and Robin." The noise came from a large besuited man with a mop of black hair. The other four men in his company laughed loudly. They were also dressed in expensive looking suits.

Terry joined in the raucous laughter before turning to me. "Steve, meet the Met's finest. The one with the big gob is Detective Inspector Wally Willow."

"Welcome to the office, Steve," Willow said. "I'll introduce you to the others later. First, what are you drinking, lad?"

"Pint of lager will be good." *I had already discovered I wasn't keen on London bitter. It wasn't a patch on Tetley Warrington's bitter.*

"Scouse, eh?"

"Yeah."

"No matter, if you're with Terry, you'll do for me."

Terry removed a large envelope from inside his suit jacket before handing it to Willow. He glanced inside, then stuffed it into his own inside pocket. It was obvious what was inside, but for what, I didn't yet know.

We stayed in the back bar all the rest of the afternoon and into the evening. I must have drunk about seven pints of lager. Terry had the equivalent of a full morning's production at a whiskey distillery. Marmalade was nowhere to be seen until just before we left. I think he had waited until the cops left.

Accompanied by much slurring, I heard him say, "Terry, okay if I go off with the lads? They are all going to a strip club and invited me along."

"Fuck me, how am I supposed to get home? Oh… fuck it, give me the keys. I'll chance it."

"Thanks, boss, sorry, boss," Marmalade said.

CHAPTER TWELVE

CLOSE SHAVE

Terry drove away from the pub, crashing gears and swerving from side to side. He assured me he was fine and had driven home in far worse states than his current inebriation. I hoped he was right but wasn't too confident. I just prayed we both got back in one piece and he didn't kill or maim any innocents.

I knew we were heading back in the direction of the Blackwall Tunnel. That idea didn't fill me with confidence as the tunnel has some severe bends in it. I guess we were about five minutes away from dicing with the tunnel walls when I saw the reflected blue lights. It was a police car and it was right behind us.

"Shit," Terry said and I felt the same. "Steve, I know this is an imposition, but I'll go to jail if I'm caught drunk driving again. Will you switch with me?"

I have no real idea why I agreed. Maybe because he asked so politely? "Yeah, pull over where it's dark so they can't see me slide over. Between those two street-lamps is ideal." I pointed to a large shady area.

I sat behind the steering wheel, waiting for a constable to arrive. It seemed ages before a thickset copper in uniform knocked at the driver's window. "Is this your car?"

"No," I said.

Terry said, "It's mine, officer."

"Did I address you?" the PC said.

"No," Terry said.

"Well then…" and left the rest hanging in midair. "You, driver, get out and stand outside the car."

I did as I was told. The copper looked me up and down before he spoke again, "Been drinking, have we?"

"A few."

He strolled to the back of the Jaguar, pulled out his truncheon and struck the rear light housing of the car. "Lookie here," he said, "a white light showing to the rear. You know that is an offence, sir, and accordingly I am obliged to administer a breath test to ascertain if you are driving under the influence of alcohol."

"That's bollocks," Terry said. "You smashed the light. I saw you."

The PC turned to his uniformed colleague. "You see me do that?"

"It was already broken." His colleague smirked.

"Terry, say nothing. It's all down to me," I said.

"Pass me the breathalyser kit, Jonesy," the first officer said.

Once it was in his hands, he carried out the routine of instructing me how to provide a sample of breath and the implications of either refusal or failure to provide a sample.

"I understand," I said and blew hard into the tube.

"Over," the officer said then arrested me, first telling me the next steps in the procedure: the provision of a blood or urine sample at the police station if I blew positive again.

He drove me to Plumstead Police Station where we were followed by his colleague, driving Terry's car. Terry had flagged down a passing taxi to get home. Before the taxi drove off, Terry said, "Call us when they are done. Rene will come and pick you up. We can arrange to get my car later."

"Thanks," was all I could think to say.

I was officially bailed at four the following morning after I had provided a specimen of urine. I was expected to return to Plumstead Police Station after the laboratory had tested the sample. There was no doubt in my mind it would prove to be positive. If I was right, that would be bail again, but to the magistrates' court this time.

I asked the desk officer if I could wait in the foyer before calling Terry for my ride back to his home and my bed. I supposed I may as well wait for an hour or so instead of rousing them this early. He said it was okay so I waited, twiddling my thumbs and feeling a little hungover. Then I had a idea and it wasn't good: *The police took my fingerprints. I will be identified as Detective Steve Hanrahan, my real identity. I must do something.*

CHAPTER THIRTEEN

IT'S ME, REGAN

No one took any notice as I stepped outside the police station. I knew what I was looking for and it took me all of three minutes to find it.

I checked my watch. It was now four-thirty in the morning. The phone at the other end rang about six times until I heard someone answer. "Reid. Who is this?"

I couldn't be heard until I fed coins into the box in the public telephone kiosk.

"Sir, it's me... Regan."

"Leave it with me," Commissioner Reid said, and that was how he finished the call after I told him about the problem. He said it calmly. I could not help but admire his sangfroid.

It was still too early to call Terry or Rene so I started walking along the high street in the direction of Woolwich. After an hour or so I found a greasy spoon café just opening. Not wishing to look a gift horse of the edible kind in the mouth, and feeling my tummy rumble, I felt I would order a full English. I don't know if she owned the gaff or was a waitress, but the tattooed woman was friendly enough. She filled me with enough confidence I wasn't going to suffer from food poisoning after I noticed how clean she looked.

"Yes, love, black pudding and the bubble too," I said in response to her queries about my breakfast order. I added, "Tea, yeah, that would be good." She went out the back and I then realised I could do with a morning newspaper. "Back in a jiffy," I yelled.

"Right you are, dear," tattoo woman called back.

I popped into the newsagents next door and bought the daily rag and a packet of fags before I returned to my seat in the caff. As usual, I scanned the back pages for news of Liverpool Football Club with no success. The London press didn't seem to believe any football team outside of London was worth a mention. I was in the middle of that idea when tattoo woman served up my breakfast. It was huge: two rashers of bacon, two sausages, two fried eggs, fried bread, black pudding, a dollop of bubble and squeak or fried left-over vegetables to a non-Cockney, plum tomatoes and some mushrooms undoubtedly from a can, two slices of toast dripping with butter, and a steaming hot mug of tea.

"Anything else?" she asked.

"Bigger trousers," I said.

"Eh?"

"These won't fit me after I eat this lot." I pointed down in the direction of my lower half.

"Funny," she said and left me alone with my banquet.

I ate it all. I was hungry but now sated. *Time to call for a lift*, I thought.

Rene picked me up in her car about thirty minutes after I called using another phone box.

"Terry says have the morning off," Rene said as I got into the front passenger seat. "You need a bath, too, judging by the smell." She smiled and she was right.

"That's what a night in the nick does for you." I smiled right back.

"Terry won't forget this, you know. You did him a big favour."

FOURTEEN

JUST DO IT

At the same time Regan was talking to Rene Culver, the Commissioner of the Metropolitan Police, Sir Edward Reid, called the Commander of the police area that included Plumstead Police Station. "Sir Edward, good morning. To what do I owe the honour?"

"Cut the crap, Bill. Eddie, to you in private."

"Okay, it must be something important, judging by your tone."

"It is, and don't ask questions."

"Right." Commander Bill Shaw stiffened up in his office chair.

"Who can you trust at Plumstead?"

"My brother in law. He's an Inspector there."

"Ideal. Now listen carefully. Last night a Steve or Steven Regan – I'll spell that, R-E-G-A-N, Romeo-Echo-Golf-Alpha-November, it's pronounced *Raygun* not *Reegan*, got it?"

"Yes, I have written it down."

"No! Destroy it. Listen and commit to memory, okay?"

"This must be important. You were about to say last night…"

"It is of the utmost importance. Last night he was nicked on a breathalyser stop by two uniforms in Plumstead. I want someone to destroy his fingerprints, then when they have done that, either get rid of the piss sample or substitute it for clean urine. Got it, Bill?"

"You sure about this?"

"Just do it. And by the way, have the A/O sent on a baton training course. He needs to be reminded about the improper use of a police truncheon."

"What's that about the arresting officer?"

"Never mind, forget that bit. Just get rid of the fingerprints and the sample. Whatever you do, just do it, no questions asked."

CHAPTER FIFTEEN

GRATITUDE

Rene dropped me off at their home in Wanstead. "You got your key?" she asked.

"Yes, thank you." I liked the way she said *your* key. I liked these people. They trusted me, and that didn't make me feel all that good.

"After you take a bath and change clothes, get a minicab to the office. The number is by the phone in the hall. Just tell them it's the Culver account so you don't need to pay the driver."

"Thanks," was all I could think to say.

Rene opened the car window and called out to me as I was making my way to the front door. "And get Pauline to rustle up some lunch before you set off, even if it's just a sandwich."

Letting myself in the front door, I heard the vacuum cleaner buzzing like an angry swarm of wasps. *I hate that noise*, I thought. Before I could start to make my way upstairs, the dreaded noise stopped. Pauline called out, "Is that you, Mister Regan?"

"It is indeed, Pauline," I shouted back. "I'm just going to take a bath."

"Okie dokie, dear. If I'm gone before you finish, I'll leave a nice chicken sandwich in the fridge for you."

"Okay, thanks."

I made my way to my bedroom and disrobed, but first I ran the bath. Back in my room, I picked out some clean clothes and lay them on the bed. Then it was time to relax in the warm water. The temperature was perfect, causing me to feel sleepy as I luxuriated in the bath's soapy bubbles. But I didn't and couldn't fall asleep because I started to think about Terry and Rene, and how kind they were to me – a stranger. Not only kind but trusting of me. *Better get used to it*, I thought. *It's all part of the lie, the grand deception. From now on, I am who I say I am. If anyone discovers who I really am, I'm probably as good as dead. I wonder if it will end up messing with my head.*

Will I wake up one day and think 'Who the fuck am I?'

At that idea I started to laugh. It caused me to slip down further in the bath so I was now submerged in bubbles and warm water. Coughing and spluttering, I raised my head above the water and heard a shout, "Are you all right up there, dearie?"

I managed a spluttered, "Yes. I'm fine, thank you." It was Pauline.

She retorted, "Good to know you haven't drowned. The chicken sandwich is in the fridge. I'm leaving now, dearie."

"Right. Thanks," was all I could utter before another bout of laughter overtook me.

I got dressed and while eating my chicken sandwich, which was delicious, I called the taxi firm to book a cab to take me to the office. Between a gob full of sandwich and my Scouse accent, the despatcher eventually figured out what I was saying.

"Okay, I got it now. On account, you say?"

"That's right."

"You from Liverpool?" she said.

"Yeah, why?"

"Nothing really. I like the Beatles and you sound a bit like John Lennon."

"Is that good?"

"Different."

"Ah, okay, my brother looks like Paul McCartney."

"Wow! You don't say."

"I do say. I just did, like."

"Funny, just like John Lennon."

Sensing she liked men chatting her up, I couldn't resist a tune. "Love, love me do, please love me do…"

She laughed. "Yeah, funny. Your cab will be with you in about thirty minutes."

"Great! Fab! Gear!"

"What does 'gear' mean?"

"Great or fab, like. Some of us say sound or boss. All means the same thing. Gear!"

"No wonder I couldn't understand you at first. It's like a foreign language. Why do you say 'like' so much?"

"Just what we do, like. It's the way we talk, but you make a good point. Liverpudlians see themselves as foreigners. The 'Republic of Liverpool' set in England, ha! Tarrah, like."

"I know that one. It means bye bye."

She put the phone down before I could reply, and I wondered if she knew I was exaggerating my Liverpool accent. I don't usually say 'like' as much as I did to her. I was just acting the part of a Liverpool scally.

The taxi driver dropped me off outside Terry's betting shop. He was the quiet type which was a relief. I had no energy left to go through the verbal shenanigans I had with the taxi firm's despatcher. He did speak briefly before I got out of the car. "On account? Is that right?"

"Yes, pal."

"That's what Slack Alice said."

"Who's that?"

"Our daytime despatcher. She's called Alice. We call her Slack Alice behind her back because…"

"Okay, mate. I get the picture."

CHAPTER SIXTEEN

BLAZING ROW

I was halfway up the stairs when I heard raised voices. It was more than an argument, more like a blazing row. It was Terry and Marmalade going at it hammer and tongs. I reached the landing at the top of the stairs when it was obvious to me they were in Terry's office. I thought better of disturbing them so waited outside, listening to the racket.

"Of course, it's all your fault. You shouldn't have got pissed in the boozer with your blagger mates," Terry yelled.

Thereafter, their voices rose exponentially with every invective, every verbal cut and thrust, each verbal dagger. I assumed I might have to burst in if it turned violent.

"Canna get pissed, now, eh?" Marmalade roared in his war-like Scottish clan impersonation of Mel Gibson in *Braveheart* but sounding way more authentic.

"Get pissed as much as you want but not when you're working as my chauffeur."

"Chauffeur! Ha! Listen at ye. I'm a driver is what I am, not some ponced-out fancy name like *show ferrr*."

That made me chuckle inside.

"As soon as that kid can drive again, he can have your job, and you will hit the high road."

"The Scouse? You dinna know sweet Fanny Andrews about him."

"I know more than you think."

At that, I sucked in my breath, wondering what was coming next.

"Such as?" the Scot demanded.

"He's recommended by a close friend of mine in Liverpool. That's good enough for me. Anyway, it's got bugger-all to do with you."

"Aye, but do ye ken him?"

"Oh, fuck off, Marmalade. Go fuck yourself."

"Last time you call me that. I've warned ye before. I will fuck off. I'm off to the pub."

The office door opened and the huge frame of Marmalade almost filled the open space, which a few seconds ago had been a solid door. He looked at me and growled. No talk, just a growl – a low Scottish growl. Then he slammed the door so hard behind him, it made me jump. I thought, *Yes, he has got a flaming temper to match his red mane.*

The door re-opened and Terry stopped short of continuing the verbal tirade on seeing me outside on the landing. "Come in, Steve. Ignore that idiot. How much did you hear?" His hands were trembling, with anger I guess.

"Terry, let's sit down inside your office. I think you need to take it steady."

"You're right, son."

Okay, as an older man, he was entitled to use 'son' as an informality, but I think he genuinely liked me as a son. *Here we go again, the guilt thing – the deceit involved*, I thought. *Toughen up, get used to it*, something or someone said inside me. *But will I? Ever? I must retain my humanity, my sanity.*

As soon as Terry sat behind his desk, he pointed to the malt whisky. "Right, you are," I said, pouring a wee dram, as Marmalade would say.

He took a swallow then said, "Better, much better," and smiled. "Okay, as I was saying, how much did you hear?"

"Not much, really. I heard you both shouting and you blaming him for what happened last night because he got pissed."

"That's about right. If he had stayed off the pop then I wouldn't have ended up driving and you wouldn't have spent last night in a police station cell."

"Suppose so."

"No suppose about it, Steve. As soon as your ban is over, I'll give him the old tin-tack and you're my new driver."

"Tin-tack?"

"Forgot you're no Cockney. Tin-tack rhymes with sack. Sack him, fire him, whatever. You become my new driver."

"You mean *show ferrr,*" I said, doing my best Marmalade parody.

"Knock it off, don't you start." He laughed. "Anyway, it's about time you had your own little flat. Let me show you what I have in mind."

"Is it far?" I asked.

"Nope, it's on the top floor of this place. And one other thing, call me Tel, not Terry, okay?"

"Gotcha, Tel," as I now did my best to adopt a Cockney accent.

He laughed out loud again.

CHAPTER SEVENTEEN

A DATE

Terry had a contractor in to renovate the top-floor flat. A new kitchen and shower room were installed along with a new bed, sofa, two armchairs, and a small dining table with four matching chairs. He went as far as kitting it out with a new colour TV set, fridge/freezer, and an electric oven with cooking rings on top. A private phone line was also installed in the name of Steve Regan. *That's good*, I thought. *I can keep in touch with Sir Edward if needed. It's safe because the bill will be in my name. I'm now thinking like the spy that I am.*

Rene played her part in choosing stuff like curtains, bedding, and the crockery. All of this kicked off those guilt trips even more. *They are good people*, I believed. As soon as the notion entered my head, I banished it. I had to if I wished to stay sane.

It took three weeks for the contractor to complete the job and before I could move in. During that time, I familiarised myself even more with Terry's business and got familiar with Margaret, the girl who blushed so prettily. She was twenty-two, a little shy, or so I initially imagined. We dated a few times before I took her back to my new flat. That was how I found out she wasn't as shy as I first thought.

I liked her... a lot. She was from Whitechapel in East London. It was from her I learnt what Cockneys meant by "going up West" - the West End of London, places like Soho for clubbing and the theatre district for shows and a good choice of eating spots. Cockneys liked "going up West" a lot, both young men and women.

Before the move into my own place I trekked across to Whitechapel one evening from Terry and Rene's home in Wanstead. I had arranged to meet Margaret outside Whitechapel Tube Station on the busy A11 main road. It was our first date. She looked gorgeous with her long blonde hair, and dressed to the nines. I suggested we go for a quick drink in the nearby Blind Beggar pub. She nodded, not saying a word, but her smile was as wide as the Thames river just a short distance away.

We spent about thirty minutes in the pub, talking about not much, except she mentioned the Kray twins a few times and told me they weren't seen as ruthless gangsters in this neck of the woods, but champions of the under-classes. I loved watching her talk and was fascinated by her Cockney accent but couldn't help imagining that George Cornell wouldn't share her attitude toward Ronnie Kray. Ronnie got done for his murder in the same pub back in 1966.

I didn't talk much. I was a bit nervous. This was the first date I'd had since my wife died and I felt I was out of practice. Besides, I was enjoying her chatting and her company. Margaret was drinking white wine. Mine was a pint of beer. I suggested we might have another one. It was then she said she would buy the next round. I was flabbergasted. "What?" I said.

She smiled a beautiful smile, paused then said, "London girls." That was all.

"What?" This was all new to me.

"It's a known fact, Steve. They've always got a pound to buy their round when it's their turn up the bar."

"Well, I never. Wouldn't catch Scouse girls doing that. By the way, that rhymes. You should turn it into a catchy little song."

Margaret smiled. We had another round and she paid. "Let's get the bus into town, okay? We can sit on top and I'll give you a guided tour of the famous London River Thames," she said as we were finishing our second drinks.

"Fine by me."

I was so pleased we did for more than one reason. The top deck of the bus was empty, so we got to sit close to each other. It was a first for me… a feeling of intimacy on a bus. Not only was she stunning looking at close range, she was also wearing the most exquisite fragrance. She smelled fantastic. "What's it called," I asked.

It was now her turn to say, "What?"

"The name of the perfume."

"Chanel No. 5."

I made a mental note.

The other reason was her promise of a guided tour. It turned out perfect. There was a full moon out and at one point on the journey, through a break in the old warehouses at Wapping, we saw the full moon reflecting in the murky waters of the River Thames. It was a romantic sight and one I didn't forget… ever. I saw it in a dream one night a little while later, but in my dream the moon was obscured by the silhouette of a man dressed all in black with a gun tucked into his waistband at his back.

The rest of the night was also perfect. We went dancing at a club in Soho to some live rock n' roll music before we had a late supper. I paid for a black cab to drop Margaret off before taking me on to Wanstead. Getting out of the cab at her front door, she said, "I hope we do this again."

"Sounds like a plan to me." I smiled, and she leaned over to kiss me.

"Goodnight, Margaret."

"Goodnight, Steve."

Making sure Margaret went in through her front door, my internal trance was broken by the sound of an irritated cab driver's voice, "Are we all done here then?"

I thought, *Jealous guy.*

CHAPTER EIGHTEEN

SAMSON TO THE RESCUE

"When are you due back at the cop shop?" Terry said.

"Tomorrow evening, seven, I think. I'll check later," I said.

"Okay, I'll come with you. Not much I can do though, as they will charge you then bail you again, but to court this time."

"Thanks, Tel, I appreciate that."

His office phone rang. "Take a seat, Steve. This might take a few minutes. It's an overseas call I'm expecting... from Hong Kong to be exact."

My ears pricked at the mention of Hong Kong. It was supposed to be Chinese Triads behind the

World Cup football match fixing. *At long last*, I thought, *A development.*

Terry was on the phone for longer than a few minutes. It was more like thirty. I sat patiently all that time but all I could hear was Terry seemingly agreeing with a lot and a few "Yes, I'll make sure you are met at Heathrow. Don't worry." But the thing that really registered was, "Yes, the Russian official will be there too."

Yes, I believed, *This must be to do with the World Cup Final betting scam. It's why I'm here. Go away guilt! I'm working.*

Now I started to really understand how to cope with undercover work. The adrenaline of the 'chase' and the sheer excitement of clandestine work pushed back any misgivings I had. *In a way sad, but true.*

Good to his word, Terry drove me to Plumstead Police Station. He waited in the public reception area while I was taken through to what I imagined was going to be the charge room, but instead I was shown into a ground floor office. The office of Inspector Perkins, I learnt as soon as he introduced himself. *What's this?* I thought.

"Mister Regan, please allow me to get straight to the point," the Inspector said. "There will be no charge resulting from your arrest a few weeks back…"

I didn't let him finish. "Why?"

"No evidence."

"What about the piss sample?"

"Gone. Disappeared."

"How?"

"That's not your concern. There is a full internal inquiry, but even if we discover the truth, it's highly unlikely you will be notified. Just be glad there's no court and no ban for you, Mr Regan. It's your lucky day."

I smiled inwardly, thinking, *No luck involved at all, my friend. And you never mentioned my fingerprints and arrest sheet had disappeared too.*

I told Terry all about it in the car. He was delighted. "Tomorrow," he said, "you will be my new *showww ferrr*." His take on Marmalade was better than mine.

Poor Marmalade, I thought. I didn't mean it. There was something about him.

The next day three things happened. Terry sacked Marmalade. He made me his new driver and I moved into the flat. *Things were on the up.*

Before I moved my things into the flat, I had a long chat with Terry in his office.

"How did Marmalade react?" I asked.

"Like always. He's got a temper on him. Loads of threats and swearing. Couldn't make out most of it because of that Scottish accent, but it didn't need an expert to pick out a lot of 'effing c's. You know the c-word that rhymes with Roger Hunt. He did say he'd 'get even,' whatever that means."

"Hmm, you need to be careful. He's got some tasty blagger friends."

"I know but they are armed blaggers who tool up with sawn-off shotguns to raid security vans full of cash. Can't see I'm their kind of target, can you?"

"Perhaps, but better to be careful."

"Yeah, I will, and something else, Steve. No one, and I mean no one, knows about any of this, not even Rene."

"What's that, Tel?" *I had an idea of what he was about to say but stayed calm inside.*

"I got involved in a betting coup, a scam re-ally. It was an inside fix on the result of the sixty-six World Cup Final. We, by that I mean an international crew, got to the Russian linesmen by offering them a huge bribe to affect the result of the match."

"Why are you telling me this?"

"Some of the Hong Kong crew and one of the Russians are flying into London soon and I want you to meet them at Heathrow, take them to their hotel, and generally babysit them. It's best if you at least know something about the whys and wherefores."

"I guess you're right. But what about the other linesman? I thought two were bribed."

"Killed. He wanted more money to keep his trap shut. We can't mess around with these Triads."

Soon, it was Friday, one of the busiest betting days with weekly-paid workers blowing their money on gambling and booze, then later facing an understandably distraught wife on their return home. Late Friday afternoons meant a lot of cash on the premises of betting shops throughout the country. Terry Culver's Turf Accountant shops were no different.

I was talking to Margaret behind the screen at the Barking shop when I glanced up to see a man dressed completely in black enter through the front door. It all happened in a flash, but I believe I first noticed the tell-tale gait - splayed-out feet. Then I saw the man's black hood covering his face and another tell – some wispy red hair sticking out a little. *Marmalade!* I saw his hand move behind him. Now he held a gun in his hand.

I wasn't the first one to make a move. It was Samson, the Irish punter's small dog. Growling and snapping, then barking loudly, it certainly caught Marmalade's attention. Samson started to bite at Marmalade's ankle and the former driver pointed the gun at the mutt. Before he could pull the trigger, the intruder got it from two fronts. Miles, Samson's elderly Irish owner and former Commando, whacked Marmalade over the head with a stool. I was watching this like it was a freeze-frame celluloid movie sequence. I certainly wasn't conscious of picking up a large, heavy glass ashtray, opening the door separating the private from public areas, then letting fly with an aim Robin Hood would have applauded. Down and out!

As I made my way to the prone intruder, Miles collected the gun and made it safe. Samson was licking Marmalade's face. I knew Margaret had a

Polaroid behind the counter, so I yelled, "Margaret, camera now."

She trotted out warily, camera in hand.

"Take a picture, please. Samson licking the idiot's face."

"Okay," she said. It whirred a while and I watched as the photo slid out. Margaret handed it to me as Marmalade started to stir.

"Throw that water on his face, Miles," I said.

Picking up a plastic bottle full of water, Miles emptied the contents on the intruder's face.

Marmalade hadn't finished spluttering when I showed him the Polaroid. "This will find its way to all your mates if you ever pull a stunt like this again or come near any of Terry's shops, his home, his family or any of his workers. Got it?"

Miles added, "That includes me and my dog."

"Sorry, Miles. I should have included the two heroes of the hour."

"Didn't do so bad yerself, Mister Regan. That's a wicked right arm you got there."

I grabbed the soaked, embarrassed would-be robber under his arms and yanked him up to his feet. Grabbing his shoulders, I spun him, so he faced the door to the street. "Go. Don't come back." Then I kicked him up the backside.

Running and pulling off his hood, Marmalade disappeared into the street outside.

On turning back to the people inside, I heard cries of, "Three cheers for Steve, Miles and Samson."

"Miles, I'll take that," I said pointing at the gun.

The uproar had just settled down when Terry appeared behind the screen, having come down from his office. "What did I miss?" he asked.

He looked puzzled as everyone present, except Terry, laughed loudly.

"I'll tell you later," I said over the hubbub.

CHAPTER NINETEEN

ENTERTAINING

A lull followed the Marmalade incident. It would be another two weeks before Terry asked me to go to Heathrow to meet the Hong Kong people. By the time he spoke to me in depth about what happened in the shop that day, he had already got different versions from all and sundry. Some told a tale of me pulling out a gun and pistol-whipping Marmalade. Others told of Miles tripping him up as he entered the shop. So, it was a case of setting the record straight when I told him the truth. Terry appeared content, amazed, and grateful on hearing me recount the full story. He did have a question for me though. "Why didn't you call the police?"

"I thought it best not to involve them. Besides, with that Polaroid we took, I don't see him ever showing his face again. He'd lose too much face."

"You're right. Nice one. One more question, Steve. Where's the gun?"

"Hidden. You never know when I may need it."

"You know how to use one?"

"Sure. I used to go to a gun club years back."

"Driver and bodyguard, eh?"

"Correct!"

"I hear you and Margaret are seeing quite a bit of each other."

"Prying or…"

"No. not prying. Just interested. She's a nice girl."

"I know."

The following Saturday evening, with Terry's query still on my mind, I used his Jaguar to collect Margaret from her parent's home in Whitechapel, taking full advantage of Terry's offer to use the Jag whenever he didn't need it. She had accepted my offer to cook for her at my flat. This would be the fifth time we had spent time together, each time better than the last. Margaret had told me she felt the same. That was when I decided to be honest with her before inviting her to my flat. No – not tell her who I really was but that I was fond of her and didn't want her believing there was a white dress and a gold ring at the end. I believed that would end our relationship, but much to my surprise, and delight, she accepted it all.

"Steve. I kind of knew this and it's not a problem. I sometimes think you are a mystery man and there's things you don't know about yourself or even who you

are. That excites me. You are definitely not boring."
That was how Margaret responded to my outburst of
honesty.

I couldn't resist my answer, knowing she wasn't offended by the F-word, again a trait of many young
London girls. "Yeah." I smiled. "Who the fuck am I?"

"As long as you are a fucking good cook, who
cares," she said after I had invited her for dinner at my
place.

Now, waiting outside her front door – we had an
agreement that her parents were not to meet me – I was
nervous once more. It was a different kind of nervous-
ness from that I felt when I met and took her for a drink
in the Blind Beggar. This was borne of a sexual frisson
– deep desire inside of me. It had been a long time since
I had been to bed with anyone.

That feeling disappeared the moment she glided
into the Jag's front passenger seat. It was the combination of the olfactory effects of Chanel No. 5, and clean
blonde hair, the short skirt riding up shorter as she got
comfortable revealing a lot of shapely thigh, but above
all, it was her smile.

"Hi, mystery man! Where are we going? On a mag-
ical mystery tour?" Margaret said.

"None of the above. My place, or had you forgot?
And what's about the bag? That's bigger than your nor-
mal handbags."

"Girl things."

"What?"

"Steve, a change of clothes, a nightie, toothbrush etcetera."

I almost choked. "You plan on stopping the night?"

"If you let me, yes."

"But…"

"You are so old-fashioned. I'm on the pill."

I was getting an education. This was a difference between living in London and living in the provinces. The 'Swinging Sixties' had largely managed to pass me by but now in the seventies, life was starting to look great.

I smiled back, engaged gear and drove the thirty minutes to my flat. During the trip, I was quiet – thinking. Margaret was fine with that as I had put a music station on the car stereo. I could see her head nodding, feet tapping along to the beat. She looked happy. *I like her honesty*, I thought. *I can have a beer too, no more driving tonight.*

She noticed my smiling at my own thoughts. "Penny for them?

"No way, not for a thousand quid."

"Ooer, sounds exciting, mister mystery man."

The dinner was fine. Steaks cooked to perfection, both medium-rare, some sautéed potatoes, mushrooms, tomatoes, and my pièce de résistance – a packet of peppercorn sauce mix which I hid from view. It was all washed down with a cheap but tasty burgundy, having persuaded Margaret to forsake her usual white wine. The conversation was light as we ate, drank and listened to an eclectic music mix on the radio including Boney M, Queen, Jimi Hendrix, Chuck Berry, Beatles and the Rolling Stones. We cracked up laughing when Little Jimmy Osmond came on singing "Long Haired Lover from Liverpool".

"It's not that long," Margaret said as she stroked the nape of my neck. "That was a great meal, Steve. Thanks."

"Look, leave the dishes. I'll do them tomorrow. Let's sit on the sofa and listen to more music."

"Great idea, but wait. I want to brush my teeth and change."

"Change into what?"

"That would be telling. Surprise, so wait, mister mystery man who can cook, and I bet that's *not all* he can do."

This was *not* the shy Margaret I once knew. I chuckled and waved her off with a nonchalant jokey wave of my hand.

She returned in about five minutes and I took one long look at the wonderful sight in front of me. Margaret was dressed in a negligée baby doll outfit. I could see her curves and other womanly bits right through the flimsy black fabric. She came around to the back of the sofa and stroked my hair. Then leaning over my shoulder, she lightly kissed my cheek, followed by her rolling over the sofa back so she was next to me with her head on my lap. "I see you like my outfit. It's no mystery what caused that to go hard." She laughed as she groped my trousers hiding my erection. "Steve, let's go to bed."

How was I to resist, and why should I?

I stood up, as did Margaret. I held out my hand and she took it, leading me to my bedroom. I followed willingly.

CHAPTER TWENTY

THIS IS HOW IT IS

We did get some sleep, but it didn't matter. It was the weekend, so no need to rise and shine, but there was a 'rise' and it made us both content as we lay in each other's arms after some more great love-making, or was it just sex.

The clock at the bedside table told me it was nine in the morning. I was feeling hungry and my stomach noises betrayed the fact.

"Listen to you," Margaret said.

"Hunger pangs. I'll make some breakfast."

"Wow! Dinner and breakfast with full service in between. You'd make a very good husband for some lucky lady, Steve," she said.

"This is how it is."

"What?"

"Let me make this crystal clear. I like you. I like you very much and you are a fantastic lover, but I can't ever see me being married."

"You're not too shabby yourself in bed, Steve."

"Thank you, and what else is there about me you like other than being a great cook?"

"Oi! Bighead, I'm sorry now I praised your cooking skills. Okay, honestly, I like this man of mystery thing about you, but you also seem vulnerable. I mean… look at those eyes…"

"What about them?"

"Sad and also great 'come to bed' eyes."

"Really? What colour are they?"

"Don't you know?"

"No, I never look at them. They're just there, like."

"Different. They are dark but different. I mean, one is tinged with green and the other tinged with a fleck of blue. They hypnotise me."

"And what's with the sad bit?"

"Oh, you know, as if something really bad happened in your life," Margaret said looking sad herself thinking about it. "Tell me. Have you ever been married?"

I paused for a few moments, reminding myself that I was now an undercover cop and sensing that guilt at what I was going to say next.

"No. Never. I don't want the commitment. I'm not ready for that. As I said, 'this is how it is.'"

"Well, that's another thing I like about you – your honesty. Many blokes would lie to me just to get what they want. But you, you're different."

I fell silent again for a moment, thinking of the irony of what she had just said.

"Hey, Margaret. We have a good time together, right? Let's just tick along as we are. You can come stay over anytime," I said but felt, *Not when I need to make private phone calls to Sir Edward.*

"I'd like that," she said. "Now, what about that breakfast?"

"Coming up. Scrambled eggs okay with you?"

"Love them, my long-haired lover from Liverpool." Margaret laughed and slapped my backside as I jumped naked out of bed.

"Great, I'll shower first," I said picking up a robe slung over the bedside chair.

CHAPTER TWENTY-ONE

CALL ME BOB

Margaret and I did tick along. She was no burden at all. She played it cool at work, just flashing the odd knowing smile at me which I of course returned in kind. We chose our moments carefully when making our arrangements to meet, whether to go out on a date or a weekend session of lovemaking. Life was so good, I almost forgot there were only ten days to go before the meet and greet at Heathrow airport. *It's time to talk to Sir Edward*, I thought.

"Sir, yes, Hong Kong Chinese, then supposedly the next day I have to meet the Russian. Terry Culver is to hold a meeting with them. I don't think even he knows where or when yet."

I was talking to Sir Edward Reid, the Met Commissioner, my contact, from the phone in the flat. I had direct dialled to his secret ex-directory number so even if someone checked my phone records, they wouldn't have a clue as to who I was talking to.

"Steve, you must drop the 'Sir' stuff. I know you are cautious, but you never know if someone is able to overhear you. From now on call me Bob, and if it's really urgent, call me Fred. Got that?"

"Got it, Bob." I heard the knight of the realm laugh.

"Steve, what we must do is covertly record this meeting."

"Agreed, but I don't know the location or time and date yet."

"Right, think on this. I have contacts at the Dorchester in Park Lane. I can swing it for a suite to be hired to accommodate this meeting, plus adjoining rooms for the Chinese and the Russian. The whole floor if necessary."

"Sounds good."

"Does Culver plan to book rooms for these guys?"

"I don't know, but don't think so. He just told me to meet and greet, then take them to their hotel."

"Let me work on this. Call me tomorrow."

"Yes, Bob."

The line clicked dead before I could replace the handset.

Things are moving at last, but this will be tricky, I thought. *Dare I talk to Terry about this? No, too risky. Oh fuck it, this'll never work without his cooperation.*

CHAPTER TWENTY-TWO

PRIVATE STUFF

It was later that day when I asked Terry to have a chat in my flat.

"What's wrong with my office, Steve?" he asked.

"It's private stuff."

"Good enough, let me finish off signing these letters and I'll be up there in a few minutes."

"Right you are, thanks," I said as I left his office and went upstairs to my flat.

I opened the door to my flat after the bell rang. It was Terry as expected, but wearing a frown, unlike his usual cheery self.

"I have a feeling I'm going to hear something I'd rather not hear."

"Terry, do you trust me?"

"I trust you with my life. Since you arrived here, I think of you as a son and so does Rene."

"That makes it all the harder to say what needs saying."

"You had better start and clue me in, then."

"First, you must trust me and not a word of all this must escape this room."

"Sounds serious."

"It is, and if anyone fucks up, me, you, and some others could get killed. I'm going to ask you to do something and I need your full cooperation for this plan to work. Are you understanding how serious all this is?"

"I am. I've never seen you like this. What's this plan?"

Over the next few minutes I laid out the plan and watched his face as the full enormity of all the ramifications ran through his mind.

"What about me? Do I go to prison?"

"I'll make sure you get full immunity from prosecution, I promise." I felt, *Shit, I hope I can.*

"Who are you, exactly?"

"I can't tell you. Please trust me."

"I must be mad… but okay, I will. I'll go along with this plan. Steve, bring that gun along. These Chinese are no idiots."

"Thanks, Tel, and remember – don't tell a soul, even Rene."

"What about Brian?"

"No one. No one at all."

"Okay. I need you to know I wouldn't do this for anyone else but you. Please don't let me down, Steve."

"I won't." I said a prayer silently before I let Terry out of the flat.

CHAPTER TWENTY-THREE

LIVERPOOL COMEDIANS

Late that night I called Sir Edward from my flat.

"You did WHAT!" the Commissioner exploded and it wasn't a question. *Oh, shit*, I thought as I gathered my composure.

"Bob, I believed it was the right thing to do and I still do. I'm here on the ground and I'm asking you to trust my judgement."

I heard a sharp intake of breath on the other end of the line and there were a few moments of icy silence. *Clearly, he's thinking.*

"I have to hand it to you, young Regan. That took some balls."

"I accept the compliment."

"Now, don't get cheeky with me, young man."

"I'm not. It's my famous Scouse sense of humour."

"If this goes pear-shaped, you'll be joining the ranks of Liverpool comedians."

"Okay, Bob. I got the picture, and anyway if that happens you won't have far to go to see me at the Palladium."

Thankfully, I heard him laugh. "You are a one-off, do you know that?"

"The world couldn't manage two of us."

"Thank God for that. And by the way, the plan can't work without the cooperation of the head security man at the Dorchester. His name is King. Write down this name and number. Call him using the name Ernest Hemingway and the agreed passwords between you is 'offside, ref' after he asks you, 'do you think it was a goal?' Got that?"

"Yes, his name and number please."

"Kenny King, oh-one-nine-three-nine-one-thousand, got it?"

"I've written it down, not that I'll forget his name. Who is he?"

"You don't need to know except he's head of security."

"Okay, Bob. I'll call him as soon as I can confirm when our guests are arriving at Heathrow."

"Right, and Steve…"

"Yes?"

"Well done."

The line was now dead.

CHAPTER TWENTY-FOUR

LIES, DECEPTION, GUILT

Rene collared me in the office the next day. "Steve, can I talk to you in private? Terry's out all day so we can use his office."

He's told her. Putting my thoughts to one side, I followed Rene for our *tête-à-tête*, fearing the worst.

Taking a chair in Terry's office, I listened closely.

"Do you know if anything's wrong with Tel?"

"No, why?"

"He's just been so serious, as if something is on his mind. I thought if anyone knows, it might be you."

"Have you asked him?"

"I said something like, 'if you have a problem, I'm all ears'."

"And?"

"And nothing. He just said, 'leave it out.' That's not like him at all."

"I'm sure it's nothing to worry about even if there is an *it*."

"I hope so, Steve. You would tell me if you knew something?"

"Of course," I lied, and sounded so convincing.

"Okay, thanks for listening to me. How's things with you and Margaret?"

"Good."

"Do I detect the sound of wedding bells?"

"Rene, you need to get your hearing tested."

"That's a lovely way of telling me to mind my own business."

"Rene, I think a lot of you and Terry, so if there is any breaking news, you two will be the first to know."

"So sweet, Steve."

Meeting over, I followed Rene back downstairs to the betting shop floor. *Lies, deception, guilt, will I ever become immune to it? I hope not.*

Rene was right. I saw Terry enter the office from the street outside. He looked like he had a ton of bricks upon his shoulders. I noticed his usual forehead creases had darkened and now looked like black grooves on a vinyl record but larger, much larger. They were accentuated against his pale, pink tinged skin. *Hold up, hold on, Tel*, I thought. *Play this right and you'll get a hold of your get-out-of-jail card. Except this is not Monopoly, it's a high-stakes poker game.*

Deciding he was best left alone, I nodded but didn't speak to him. I didn't think he saw me, but before he started to ascend the stairs he turned and said, "Steve, pop up and see me in five, will you?"

"Okay," I said and left it at that.

Margaret walked over to me, whispering, "All okay with you two?"

"Fine," I murmured back.

I gave Terry more than the requested five minutes before I entered his office.

"Sit down, Steve."

My bum had barely touched the seat when Terry said, "I got flight details. All of them. Two coming in from Hong Kong and one from Moscow."

"Hong Kong?

"The Chinese Triads."

"Shit," I said.

"Exactly. This lot are into it all. Betting, drugs, sex trafficking, the works. So, this plan of yours better be good."

"It is." *I don't have one yet until I meet with the guy at the Dorchester.*

"Good, because they also kill people who cross them."

"How many of them?"

"Five and the Russian."

"Five on two flights from Hong Kong and one from Moscow?"

"Correct. The Moscow flight and one of the Hong Kong flights arrive at almost the same time. The second Hong Kong flight arrives about three hours later."

"Okay. I'll meet and greet the Hong Kong guys from the first flight, and the Russian, then take them to the Dorchester."

"Dorchester?"

"Never mind. Don't ask. Trust me, please."

"I do, Steve, but I'll be as happy as Larry when this is done."

"Me too."

Terry handed me a piece of paper with the flight details and passenger names written on it.

"Thanks. If you don't mind, I have some arrangements to make…" I saw Terry about to speak. "Tel, just leave it to me, okay."

"Okay, Steve. I do trust you."

On leaving Terry's office, I went up to my flat and made a phone call, dialling oh-one-nine-three-nine-one thousand. Someone picked up but said nothing.

"Mister King, it's Ernest Hemingway here," I said.

"Do you think it was a goal?" a man inquired.

"Offside, ref," I said.

"Kenny King here, Mr Hemingway," he said in a very clipped posh voice.

"When can I come and meet you?"

"Come to the hotel at seven sharp tomorrow morning. And wear a suit. I hear you prefer, shall we say, the casual look."

"See you then." I put down the receiver and thought, *Arsehole*.

CHAPTER TWENTY-FIVE

BOX

The next morning, I made my way to the Dorchester Hotel in Park Lane, making sure I arrived dead on the dot of seven. As I made my way to the front of the eight-storey building, finished in the nineteen-thirties, I admired the façade of one of the most expensive and prestigious hotels in London. I felt, *It sure beats the Adelphi in Liverpool.*

That theory became reinforced when I spotted the man standing under the ornate canopy covering the grand entrance and its two revolving doors. One for entry and the other for exit. He had a rigid military bearing and looked magnificent in his long grey tunic-style dress coat, all topped naturally enough with a top hat. I bade him a good morning which he responded to by doffing his hat with the slightest of touches to the brim, then uttered, "Good morning, sir," in a rich bass voice.

As I made my way towards the front desk, my thoughts were disrupted by a familiar high-pitched posh British accent. "Good morning, Ernest, how are you today?"

I was tempted to affect my best scally Scouse but instead I said, "Good, thank you, Kenny," in my native Liverpool accent which sounded more like John Lennon or Paul McCartney than a scally.

Mr Kenny King showed me into a security office just off the front desk. There, he introduced me to two sharply dressed men who seemed to be wearing expensive suits. They made my new off the peg suit from Burtons look shabby. "This is Steve Regan, men," he said. "You may see him in the hotel in the next few days or even next week, but just ignore him and anyone else with him."

"Yes, sir," both men said in unison.

I was believing, *This all sounds very military-like and King didn't introduce them by name. I think there's more to King than meets the eye.*

King opened up a drawer in the office table, pulled out some kind of ID on a lanyard and handed it to me. "Put that around your neck, Regan."

"Okay," I said and saw it was an identity pass with VIP SECURITY printed on it.

"Now, follow me for the guided tour," King commanded.

He's not getting a 'sir' from me, the prick, I thought as I followed him out of the security office.

We rode the lift to the top floor penthouse level in silence. As we got out, King said, "This is the Harlequin Penthouse. It's our largest roof suite and as the brochure states, 'Glowing with glamour and celebrity intrigue, our suite promises pure, bespoke luxury in the hands of unparalleled service,'" and I detected the slightest smile. This lift was exclusive to guests accommodated in this suite so on exiting the lift, one was transported into what seemed like another world. One of unadulterated luxury and fine taste.

"Take a look around. Take your time," King said.

I did and found a private terrace with views of Hyde Park, two large bedrooms, and a dining room for eight. It blew my mind but I acted nonchalant. "Yeah, it's nice," I said.

"Nice? Is that all?"

"Oh, okay then, it's okay."

"Hmmph!" King uttered.

I felt it better to humour him. "How much a night?"

"A lot, but not your concern. My department will pick up the tab."

Department? I thought. *This guy is no ordinary head of security. I must make a mental note of that – department. Strange choice of word.*

What was also strange was he suddenly got friendly as if he realised he'd made a *faux pas*.

"You're in luck. The Eisenhower Suite is empty. It's part of history. It's where General Eisenhower planned the Normandy invasion. Come, I'll show you."

"Yes, nice. Thanks." I thought, *He's trying to deflect me.*

I followed King to a different floor where he let us into the Eisenhower Suite using a pass key. It was also impressive, but less so than the last one.

"Pull up a chair, Regan, and let's talk about the arrangements."

I sank into the sheer luxury of an armchair close to the huge fireplace as King settled into the matching sofa opposite me. Before we got around to the important arrangements, I felt bold enough to ask a direct question. "You're not just head of security here, are you?"

"Yes and no," King said and I was a little surprised he had opened up. My next gambit was one of silence, hoping he would elaborate.

"We have top people from all over the world stay here. Money people, influencers, politicians, heads of business, some good and some not so good. Some even wish to do harm to this country..." He hesitated but I said nothing. "Yes, I work here but I also work for Box."

I knew that Box was code for MI5, the domestic arm of Britain's Security Services.

"I see, and you and Sir Edward sometimes work together?"

"Again, yes and no. It's more Scotland Yard's Special Branch."

He shook my hand after we had finalised the arrangements. I felt differently about him now. The rest was up to me, now knowing what our arrangements were for the visit of the Chinese Triads and the Russian.

Not forgetting Terry, he was a vital cog in this scheme.

CHAPTER TWENTY-SIX

BRIEFING TERRY

In three days our 'guests' were arriving at Heathrow so now was the time to brief Terry. I asked him to come up to my flat for a meeting.

"Thanks, Tel, before we start, I can confirm you have full immunity from prosecution but on one condition."

"And that is?"

"You do exactly what I ask of you. Nothing more and nothing less. If there's any deviation from the plan, your immunity disappears like…"

"A snowflake in hell?" Terry said.

"Yeah, or like disappears… like a man overtaken by an avalanche."

"Got it, Steve. Carry on."

"One, I'm not your driver. I'm your business associate *cum* bodyguard."

"Right."

"Two, you pretend you paid for the suite and rooms at the Dorchester, okay?"

"Yes."

"Three, you must get them talking about the fix at the sixty-six final."

"Of course."

"Four, no one, but no one finds out about this plan."

"Okay."

"Five, you must seem relaxed at all times."

"Yes."

"Six, do you pray?"

"What?"

"You heard me. I don't boil my cabbages twice."

"Cabbages?"

"A Scouse saying. Do you pray, I said?"

"I will."

"Good. Say one for both of us. Get to the Dorchester before me. Check in using your real name. The reservations have been made and paid for. Once I have got the Chinese and the Russian checked in, I will call your room to tell you where to go for the meeting."

"Is that in the Dorchester too?"

"It is."

Terry left my flat looking serious. I was now left to my thoughts. *Not long now. Margaret wants to see me and I want to see her. I know soon this Dorchester thing will be resolved one way or another. I may as well*

relax as best I can. Who knows? I may never see Margaret again after the plan is executed. That reminds me, I must check that weapon I took from Marmalade.

CHAPTER TWENTY-SEVEN

OMENS

The day before I was expected to go to Heathrow, things changed. I hoped they were lucky omens. I had told Terry to get the Jaguar checked over before I set off. The last thing the plan needed was for the car to break down. Good job I did. The mechanic found an oil leak in the transmission, easily fixed, but on checking further he found serious wear and tear to the transmission's innards. A new gear box had to be ordered. Plan B!

I made the call from my flat to Sir Edward's private number, but this time I addressed him as Fred, not Bob. "Fred, we have a problem."

"What, exactly?"

I told him about the problem with Terry's Jaguar.

"Let me think. Call me back in five minutes."
He hung up.

During the five minutes, I had another idea
about the plan. *Do they speak English? Chinese
and Russian, yes, but that's no fucking good to
me.*

I called again. "Fred, another problem. We
need two interpreters. One Chinese and a Russian."

"Fuck, Steve. Left that a bit late," Sir Edward
said. *That's the first swear word I've heard him
say,* I thought.

"Yeah, sorry. Only just thought about it."

"Okay, no sweat. The Chinese and the Russian
will be met by two limos. Two stretched Mer-
cedes. A contact of mine owns the limo company
at Heathrow. All I need from you are names and
flight details. Do you have them handy?"

"Yes." I read the details out over the phone
then paused. "The interpreters?"

"Chinese Mandarin or Cantonese?"

"No idea."

"They are Hong Kong Chinese, right?"

"Yes."

"Good chance they will speak Cantonese.
Leave it with me, Steve. Once I get that sorted, I

will instruct them to page you at the Dorchester, understood?"

"Them?"

"Russian and Chinese, two interpreters."

"Okay. Good job one of us is thinking straight."

"Steve, get a grip. Just do it, okay?"

"I will."

The private line rang in the Dorchester's security office. King picked up, "King."

"Reid here. Make sure Box has two interpreters for the Regan meeting. One Russian and one Cantonese, even better if the Chinese interpreter can speak Mandarin as well."

"Done."

CHAPTER TWENTY-EIGHT

THE MEETING

Sir Edward did a fine job in ensuring his pal's limo drivers got the Chinese and the Russian safely to the Dorchester. On checking in, they were unaware their every movement was being monitored by King's security team. Four of the Chinese decided to use the two bedrooms in the suite. The other plus the Russian had separate rooms on the second floor.

Terry and I had been at the Dorchester an hour before our 'guests' arrivals. King paged me and I took the call on a house phone in the grand lobby. On telling me all were in place I paged the interpreters to meet me at the front desk. "Okay, Tel. Let's do it."

He threw back his shoulders, took a deep breath and said quietly, "'Once more unto the breach, dear friends, once more; Or close the wall up with our English dead."

"Fuck me, Tel. That's a bit over the top."

"Shakespeare, you Scouse git."

"I know that," I said with relief as it showed Terence Patrick Aloysius Culver was up for it.

I saw a man and woman approach the front desk. I couldn't hear what was said but I saw the receptionist point over to me, on which the couple walked over to me and Terry.

"Mr Regan?" inquired the woman with a distinct Russian accent.

"Yes. This is Terry Culver. And your friend is?" I nodded to the Chinese man.

"Lee Chen, the Cantonese interpreter and I am Mrs Olga Smith, Russian interpreter."

"Pleased to meet you both. Permit me to make a phone call. Please wait here and you too, Terry. I will return shortly."

I spun on my heels and headed for King's office. I knew from King the limo drivers had reported to him all the foreigners spoke some English.

King was expecting me. He had his desk phone off the cradle and held it out to me. "I'll dial as I know the internal numbers," he said.

Three short calls later, I left his office, but first thanked him for his assistance, before re-joining Terry, Mrs Smith and Mr Chen.

The lift exclusive to the rooftop suite residents was ready on the ground floor and waiting for us. King had given me an override code for the lift. I called up to the penthouse using an intercom on the wall next to the lift.

One of the four Hong Kong guys answered. Chen spoke to him and got the okay to come up. We ascended to the penthouse and walked straight through to the dining table. "Is it okay if I send the lift down again for your friend and the Russian?" I said to the tallest of the Chinese guys.

He looked blank for a second. Mr Chen started to interpret but after a few Chinese syllables, the tall Chinese held up his hand. "I understand English. Yes, send down for them." He turned to Terry. "Mister Culver, delighted to see you again. And who is this man?" He pointed at me.

"Steve Regan, my business associate. And this is Mr Chen and Mrs Smith in case we need an interpreter."

"Mr Regan looks more like a bodyguard."

"He is, but also my associate. He knows all of my business, including why you are all here in London."

"Really? Very well, Terry. It's none of my business anyway unless…" He left the veiled threat hanging… unsaid.

"Steve, this is Wang Su."

"Good to meet you," I said and went to offer my hand to the tall Chinese man, but he ignored it.

"Yes," was all he said with no trace of emotion, before introducing the other Chinese men with a perfunctory hand gesture. "These men are my associates and bodyguards."

"Mr Su, are you ready for our discussions? I ask out of courtesy as you had a long flight," Terry said.

"We talk okay. I sleep on the flight. We all sleep. Business class. Anyway, we need to have quick talk before the Russian gets here."

We all moved into the dining area to take our seats for the talks. "Just wait," Su said.

"What is it?" I said.

"Interpreters work for you and Terry, yes?"

"They do and they are one hundred percent discreet."

"Good," Su said, adding, "Terry, do you know the Russian is demanding an extra one hundred thousand dollar for his part in the Wembley fix?"

"No. If that's true, he's a greedy bastard."

"I agree. Perhaps he does not know his Russian colleague disappeared without trace," Su said, adding, "Did you know he's on the official referee list for the next World Cup in West Germany in 1974?"

"No, but that means he's worth more to us as a ref than a linesman."

"Correct! That's why I propose we humour him and grant him the extra one hundred thousand dollar. We all agree?"

"Yes, makes sense," Terry said. "Steve, your money is in this so what do you say?"

"I agree too," I said, thinking, *Tel's playing a blinder – the game of his life.*

"Right, that's it. We wait for Russian and my other bodyguard to enter," Su said, picking up an apple from the fruit bowl and pouring freshly made coffee. "One more thing, Terry, may I express my sincere gratitude for the lavish accommodation you arranged for our short trip to London. Perhaps you and Mr Regan will join me and my men at the Mayfair Casino following our meeting?"

"We'd be delighted," Terry said.

CHAPTER TWENTY-NINE

THE RUSSIAN

The Russian and the last member of Su's bodyguard team entered the suite and I invited them to take a seat around the dining table. Su commenced the introductions including me, the two interpreters, and re-introducing Terry as a courtesy. Su chose to omit all his entourage from these introductions, reinforcing the sense that he was the boss and the remaining Chinese were his lackeys.

The Russian was called Alexei Kazak. He too seemed to have a good grasp of English, making the last-minute decision to use the interpreters unnecessary.

"Down to business, Alexei. What's this about you wanting extra money for the fix at Wembley in sixty-six?"

"Mr Su, I am worth a lot more to you now I'm on the referee list for the next World Cup. As a referee, I can influence the result a lot more ways than is possible as a mere linesman," the Russian said.

"I understand that but here is the thing. We are a team. I do my bit in Hong Kong and throughout Asian betting syndicates. Terry, with his vast contacts, helps lay off the bets to avoid any suspicion of a betting coup. You only do what you are told to do."

"But…"

"No buts, Alexei. That makes me angry. The bottom line is we can get anybody to do our bidding. Any official from a poor country, just like we did in Mexico in 1970."

I looked at Su's face. There was no expression at all and nothing to show his anger. A silence followed until the Russian spoke once more. "Perhaps if…"

He didn't finish the sentence. Su looked at one of his bodyguards then nodded in the direction of the Russian. I heard the silenced spit of a gun. Looking up, I saw one of the Chinese bodyguards gripping a pistol with a silencer mounted on it.

I started to fumble for my revolver but Mr Chen beat me to it by drawing his own 9 millimetre automatic. Without hesitation, he shot the Chinese gunman. Before the other bodyguards could draw weapons, Chen and Mrs Smith were pointing their guns at the Chinese. By now, I had also drawn my gun and pointed it at Su.

Chen used a phone on the dining room wall to make a call. "Mr King, your presence is required and we need a removal team."

Who are these people? I thought.

Terry was in shock. He was totally motionless and without expression. Keeping my gun trained on Su, I said, "Mr Chen, search Su and the other men for any weapons. Mrs Smith, please keep your gun trained on them while your colleague conducts the search."

It took Chen about three minutes to carry out a thorough search. "All clear, Mr Regan," he said just as King entered the suite.

First, he checked the shot Russian and the Chinese for vital signs. "Both dead," he said before using the wall phone. "Removals, two – first class – expedited. And an extraction team for four also expedited," he said.

CHAPTER THIRTY

DEBRIEFING

Before the debriefing took place, I made sure Terry got home and swore him to secrecy about the events at the Dorchester, reminding him of the immunity promise. I needed to assure King that was the right thing to do. He reluctantly agreed with me.

The debriefing took place in Sir Edward Reid's private conference room at Scotland Yard only hours after the Dorchester shootings. The only introduction necessary was that of the Home Secretary, Charles Bennion, because the other attendees all knew each other. They included, me, King, and the two interpreters Chen and Smith who I correctly guessed worked for the same department as King.

Sir Edward commenced by telling all present that Su and the other Chinese men were all members of a

Hong Kong Triad gang now incarcerated in a secret location.

At that point, I raised my hand. "Sir, I assume they will be prosecuted for the sixty-six World Cup betting scam, seeing we have the evidence from the Dorchester tape-recording?"

"Steve, I will deal with that last. You may be surprised to learn the Prime Minister knows about you and your deeds. In fact, Mister Bennion will accompany you to Chequers to meet the PM first thing in the morning."

At that, I glanced at my watch and saw it was two in the morning. "Very well, sir, but I have no change of clothes or shaving kit."

"Mr King will take care of that. He has graciously arranged for you to stay the rest of the night in the penthouse suite seeing it has been, shall we say, vacated."

"It's cleaned up now. So, no dead bodies. The beds were never slept in so you can take your pick. There's toiletries in the bathroom and first thing, I'll find you a suit to fit you and a clean shirt," King said.

"Okay, sounds good. Sir Edward, am I assured the immunity against prosecution regarding Terry Culver is a definite thing?"

"Absolutely. His cooperation went a long way to ensuring this matter was concluded successfully," Sir Edward said.

"Thank you," I said.

"Good. I think we are done here. Remember this: none of this happened," Sir Edward said.

King was as good as his word. After a great night's sleep in the suite, a soak in the bath, and a shave using the kit supplied by the Dorchester, he turned up with two suits and clean shirts, clean Y-fronts, and a tie for me to try on. The first suit was a perfect fit and much better quality than my Burton's suit. It was dark blue with a faint vertical white line. On looking at the label, I read 'Gieves & Hawkes,' and nearly fainted imagining the price.

By the time I met King down in the lobby, I felt like a million dollars. "Thanks, I love it," I said.

"Keep it as a memento."

"Wow, thanks, I will."

"Your driver awaits you. Have fun at Chequers."

Before leaving, I shook his hand warmly. "Thanks for everything, you're not an arsehole at all."

"Only sometimes, Steve. You take care now."

A black official government Jaguar awaited me outside the hotel. The capped chauffeur opened the rear passenger door for me where I climbed in to sit next to the Home Secretary, Mr Bennion.

"Change of plan, Mr Regan. We are meeting the PM at Buck Palace so we will be there in a few minutes."

"Buckingham Palace? Where the Queen lives?"

"That's the one. Her Majesty wishes to meet you, as does the PM."

I was shown into an anteroom with huge chandeliers overhead. The Home Secretary introduced me to a man I recognised – the Prime Minister. "Good morning, Mr Regan," he said. On returning his greeting, he added, "Here's the form – on presentation to The Queen, the correct formal address is 'Your Majesty' and subsequently 'Ma'am,' okay?"

"Yes, no problem, Prime Minister."

"Sir will do, Regan."

"Yes, sir." My knees were knocking. This was far worse than mixing with Chinese Triads.

Suddenly, two large doors opened and were held ajar by liveried butlers. Three Corgi dogs ran out and started to snap at my ankles. The PM calmly said, "Ignore the little beasts but if they bite, kick them… slyly."

I smiled at the idea as we entered a large drawing room with the Queen seated on a slightly raised platform.

A private secretary was standing alongside the platform. He said, "Your Majesty, the Prime Minister, the Secretary of State for the Home Department and Mister Steven Regan crave your attendance."

I was thinking, *I don't crave anything. I've been summoned to be here.*

Then the Queen spoke in that unmistakeable cut-glass voice. "Prime Minister, gentlemen, please be seated."

We sat on chairs arranged in front of the Queen's podium and waited.

"Sir Edward Reid has been kind enough to supply me with the full details of what happened at the Dorchester Hotel. I have therefore asked for you all to meet me here as there are certain ramifications arising from the incident. There are sensitivities at play. Having discussed all aspects of this case, I must request that no one says or does anything that would lead to the discovery of this secret: England's biggest sporting secret. A secret so shocking it could taint the image of British sport irreversibly if it were ever divulged.

"Please do not underestimate the prestige and pride involved in the England team winning the 1966 Jules Rimet World Cup trophy. The last thing anyone wants is the conspiracy theorists to have a field day spreading all sorts of rumours. Or as my husband said to me, 'those left-wing loonies.' So, with great reluctance, Mr Regan, there will be no one prosecuted for their activities in the betting fraud. It is therefore essential you and others in the know keep this secret and take it with you to the grave. None of this diminishes the high regard you are held in, Mr Regan, and I am sure you will go on to have an extraordinarily successful police career. Before you leave, Mr Regan, are you in a position to inform me of the precise nature of this football betting fraud?"

"Ma'am, yes," I said. "I mean, Your Majesty. The game was manipulated by bribing the two Russian linesmen. The referee, a Swiss national, was above reproach and incorruptible anyway, so the Hong Kong syndicate got at the two Russians. The first fix was to ensure the match lasted more than ninety minutes. In other words, into extra time. One of the Russians enabled that because in the lead up to the German equaliser, he overlooked an obvious foul by one of the German attackers, so allowing play to continue, leading to Germany's second goal."

"I see," the Queen said. "Was there more than one corrupting influence or act?"

"Ma'am, yes. The syndicate wanted to make sure England won by a two-goal margin for spread betting purposes. They did that once again with the bribes paid to the linesmen. When England's Geoff Hurst's shot struck the underside of the bar, we now know the linesman believed the ball had not crossed the whole of the line on the downward rebound. He was about to signal for a 'no-goal' to aid the referee but kept his flag down when he remembered his instructions. Instead, he pointed his flag to the centre circle indicating it was a valid goal. One can see that slight initial hesitation on his part if one watches the replay."

One? I thought. *I never say one, I say 'you.' Bloody hell, Regan.*

"How interesting. Thank you all for coming to see me at such short notice," Her Majesty said.

That was it. We were all dismissed. What next?

CHAPTER THIRTY-ONE

EPILOGUE

There were some decisions I had to make about my future and some loose ends to tie up. I disappeared for two weeks in Spain, renting a cottage high up in the mountains of the Pyrenees. The cool air, local food and wine helped unwind me. They certainly cleared my head.

I didn't have many belongings and they were all at the flat above Terry's betting shop. I called him to ask they be placed in storage and make sure a red blanket was included with my stuff – my daughter, Rose's bed blanket, but I didn't tell him that. He readily agreed, but queried if I was going to visit him and Rene. I told him I didn't think so. It was best we made a clean break. He also told me he had been warned to 'keep the secret' or his immunity would be revoked. I knew that was bullshit. That was the last thing they would do, otherwise 'the secret' ceases to be a secret, but I didn't tell him that. Not that it matters now because a few months after I spoke to him, he died from a heart attack. I decided not to go to the funeral. Brian Barker also died, taking his role in 'the secret' to the grave.

Margaret was history, almost. I did send her some Chanel No. 5 perfume with a note attached – FROM YOUR MYSTERY MAN. There was no more contact between us. It was part of the new life I decided to embark on – an undercover cop: no ties, no funerals, no love tangles. Indeed, I only contact my own family over the phone. It's the price I'm willing to pay to be the best undercover cop possible.

I called Sir Edward soon after returning from Spain. I told him my decision about my future work. "I'm going to carry on policing in the south and not return to Liverpool."

"Good to hear," he said. "I happen to know you'll be undercover again soon on Operation Perfume, a drugs thing, so start growing your hair and a beard."

"I will, Bob." I chortled, unable to resist it.

"Steve, I'll make sure you have a criminal record in the name Steve Regan with your fingerprints attached. Don't want a repeat of Plumstead, do we? That means your police service record in your real name and the fingerprints will disappear."

"Great, but no prison time. Just a drug bust for a small amount of marijuana and maybe a couple of minor assaults."

"Why no prison time?"

"They'd soon suss me out if I tried to bullshit about that. Everyone knows someone inside the nick."

"Steve, you will make one heck of an undercover cop. Take care and stay safe, my good friend."

THE END

AFTERWORD

There are currently four books in this series with a fifth planned – a sequel:

The Secret

Who The F*ck Am I?

Dilemma

Rivers of Blood

Now you have read *The Secret*, I hope you enjoyed the read and meeting Steve Regan.

Perhaps, you will now go on and read the other books in the *Steve Regan Undercover Cop Thriller* series. I hope so and the opening chapters follow of the next book in the series *Who The F*ck Am I?* I ask you try not to be deterred by that title. There is a valid reason behind it – it refers to the identity confusion often experienced by undercover cops. I know as I was one.

Before you read the excerpt, please also note I wrote about my real undercover days in my memoir <u>*Undercover: Operation Julie – The Inside Story.*</u> The book's adaption is now in development as a feature film.

If you would like to follow news about my books or the film, you may <u>subscribe to my newsletter here</u>.

Excerpt from Who The F*ck Am I?

Prologue

The following story is set in 1976. Back then, few people knew of the existence of GCHQ. Perhaps some vaguely knew it had connections to Bletchley Park and the cracking of the Enigma Code during World War Two. The end of that war saw the beginnings of the Cold War. It is then that the work of GCHQ expanded.

GCHQ, as the Government Communications Headquarters is better known, is housed in Cheltenham, Gloucestershire, England. Most people know it as the eyes and ears   of the United Kingdom government. Some know it as "spooksville," using the Americanism of "spook" rather than the British "spy." It employs "spies in the sky" as well as other sophisticated eavesdropping devices to monitor activities deemed to be injurious to the state or its allies. Its work, of necessity, is shrouded in secrecy.

What is not generally known is this organisation is also tasked with assisting in intelligence gathering to combat serious organised crime. Just like invisible eyes and ears, it oversees many law enforcement activities including police and Customs undercover operations. It oversees in the sense it watches and listens and gathers intelligence. To be precise, one department holds this brief – the Composite Signals Organisation (CSO).

The employees at GCHQ may as well have no name. They are faceless civil servants, UK government employees. They are not spies nor are they law enforcement officers. Some, like an anonymous middle-aged man I will call Jack, are frustrated cops. They see and hear of the exciting adrenaline fuelled lives of the men and women in the field. They marvel at the skills deployed by the undercover operatives living duplicitous lives and the inherent danger they place themselves in. Jack was fascinated by all of that. Jack knew he was good at his job within CSO and was content to play a role in the fight against crime and terrorism; a desk bound role that fulfilled him until he heard some terrible news from an old friend.

Chapter One

The Canadian could be an assassin. For sure, a big player dealing in vast quantities of heroin and cocaine. Bolivia is the source of the cocaine powder. It arrived into his control in an almost one hundred percent form. By the time it reached the streets of London it became a changed beast. If lucky, you may have had a purity of forty-five percent.

He did not control the chain of distribution all the way to street-level dealers. No need for that. Way too risky and more importantly, by the time he sold a one pound 'weight' to Steve Regan, he had made a hand-some profit.

Regan is the British man talking to the Canadian in a Liverpool nightclub in 1976. Coke, charlie or snow, to use some of its names, remained the preserve of the wealthy in 1976. Expensive, but popular with rock stars. A massive market and a huge opportunity for profit existed in Britain.

The deal had been laid out on the table. The Cana-dian and Regan became parties to a conspiracy to import serious weights of cocaine into Britain.

The Canadian's mood changed. Why? Not clear to Regan at all. Without him revealing too many details, the Canadian had impressed the Brit with the plan.

- Bolivia – check!
- Go-fast boat in place – check!

- Air hostess to bring the contraband into Britain – check!
- Prices and discounts for quantity – check!

Snap! The mood did change, and how!

"Are you guys cops?"

Wham! This question hit Regan like a vivid lightning strike from a clear blue sky. The words rolled around inside his head like thunderclaps.

A simulated assassination followed. A double tap from a silenced semi-automatic pistol favoured by professional hitmen the world over. A close-range execution.

He raised one hand next to Regan's head. The Canadian pointed his joined forefinger and middle finger in imitating a gun. The fingers touched the Regan's skin.

He silently mouthed the silenced spitting sound as two imaginary shells splattered brains out of the gaping exit wounds at the far side of Regan's head.

Pop! Pop!

This is personal, thought Regan.

Welcome to Steve Regan's world, the world of an undercover cop, identity confusion; a world with the slimmest of hold on reality or his true identity. He moves chameleon-like in the underworld mixing with those who inhabit dark places.

He is a man more likely to say, "Who the fuck am I?" when catching his reflection in a mirror, and most unlikely to utter a polite, "who am I?"

ABOUT THE AUTHOR

Stephen Bentley is a former UK police Detective Sergeant, pioneering undercover cop, and barrister (criminal trial attorney). He is now a freelance writer and an occasional contributor to Huffington Post UK on undercover policing, and mental health issues.

His bestselling memoir, 'Undercover: Operation Julie - The Inside Story,' is a frank and fascinating insight into his undercover detective experiences during Operation Julie - an elite group of detectives who successfully investigated one of the world's largest drug rings. It has now been adapted for a feature film.

Stephen also writes crime fiction in a fast-paced plot-driven style including the Steve Regan Undercover Cop Thriller and the Detective Matt Deal Thriller series.

One of his short stories, 'The Rose Slayer,' won the SIA murder mystery competition in 2018, and has now been published in a multi-author anthology of murder mystery short stories, titled 'Death Among Us.'

His fiction draws heavily on his law enforcement background adding that ingredient of authenticity about which the legendary Raymond Chandler opined, "Fiction in any form has always intended to be realistic," when writing about "the detective story" in his essay 'The Simple Art of Murder'(1950). Stephen subscribes to that school of thought.

When he isn't writing, Stephen relaxes on the beaches of the Philippines with his family where he now lives, often with a cold beer and a book to hand.

You may find him on Twitter as @StephenBentley8 or connect with him at https://www.stephenbentley.info/ where you may subscribe to his mailing list.

ALSO BY STEPHEN BENTLEY

NON-FICTION

Undercover: Operation Julie – The Inside Story

How to Drive Like an Idiot in Bacolod

FICTION

Standalone

Comfort Zone: A Tale of Suspense

Death Among Us: An Anthology of Murder Mystery Short Stories (multi-authors)

The Detective Matt Deal Thrillers

Mercy

Mayhem - Coming Soon

The Steve Regan Undercover Cop Thriller Series

The Secret

Who The F*ck Am I?

Dilemma

Rivers of Blood

CPSIA information can be obtained
at www.ICGtesting.com
Printed in the USA
BVHW071438310820
587680BV00003B/507